Chasing Shadows

This is a work of fiction. Names, characters, places, and incidents either are the product of the author's imagination or are used fictitiously. Any resemblance to actual events, locales, organizations, or persons, living or dead, is entirely coincidental and beyond the intent of either the author or the publisher.

Chasing Shadows
TOP SHELF
An imprint of Torquere Press Publishers
PO Box 2545
Round Rock, TX 78680
Copyright 2012 by Jez Morrow
Cover illustration by Alessia Brio
Published with permission
ISBN: 978-1-61040-306-1

www.torquerepress.com

All rights reserved, which includes the right to reproduce this book or portions thereof in any form whatsoever except as provided by the U.S. Copyright Law. For information address Torquere Press. Inc., PO Box 2545, Round Rock, TX 78680.
First Torquere Press Printing: April 2012
Printed in the USA

If you purchased this book without a cover, you should be aware that this book is stolen property. It was reported as "unsold and destroyed" to the publisher, and neither the author nor the publisher has received any payment for this "stripped book".

**If you liked Chasing Shadows,
you might enjoy:**

Bite by Sean Michael

Codes and Roses by Julia Talbot

Fur and Fang by Sean Michael and BA Tortuga

Touching Evil by Rob Knight

Chasing Shadows

Chasing Shadows
by Jez Morrow

Torquere Press Inc.
romance for the rest of us
www.torquerepress.com

Chasing Shadows

Prologue

The she-wolf paced atop the ruined levee. The waters that set her free were receding into a stinking wasteland. Her shaggy coat was clotted with mud. Her legs were black with it. Somewhere amid the stench her nose picked up an irresistible scent. Suddenly, urgently, she was digging in the muck. The bones called to her. She uncovered them, fresh and vibrant as a new kill. She gnawed on them with a hunger beyond hunger while spectral figures of men in flat boats plied the flooded streets. Their haunting calls and the weak responses from the stranded went on and on throughout the days and nights.

The bones kept her fed for a turn of the moon, and though she was not in heat this season, she felt a fullness in her womb.

Nine months later she gave birth to a single pup.

The seasons changed, and a male wolfdog came to court her. Though her pup had already grown bigger than either his mother or her beau, the pup ran away when they snarled at him to go.

Full grown and restless, the lone wolf crouched along a footpath that wound through a ragged park of broken trees. A woman, neither young nor old, walked the path. A bitch followed her of her own will.

The bitch saw him, stopped, and woofed.

The woman turned around. She saw where the bitch was looking, and she spoke to him in that complex noise humans made. The wolf could tell she meant no harm.

He approached the woman, his head down, hackles down. He touched his nose to her leg. He inhaled the scent of blood.

There was a scratch on her leg. He licked it.

As he tasted the blood, he heard the words. "You're not going to eat me, are you?"

Words!

Awareness struck like a bolt of lightning.

Language exploded in his mind. A flood of knowing overwhelmed him with sudden pain, like a tourniquet released too fast and forcing empty blood vessels open. Needles of agony stabbed his whole being with his awakening. It was too much. Too much knowing, and he wasn't ready to take it in. He knew everything she knew. He sagged under the torrent of knowing.

She broke contact.

The sounds from her mouth made sense now. She was saying carefully, "Okay, ya know what, honey? We're walking away now. We don't want no trouble, ya know what I'm saying?"

He swayed where he was, reeling from what he'd seen in their brief connection. Then he crawled away from the footpath, trying to process the incredible deluge. The pieces of knowledge he did retain were outlandish, stunning in the truest sense of the word. He was stunned. He *knew*.

He remembered what he was. Who he had been.

And he knew the year was 2007!

Two Thousand and Seven!

The patrolman walked the night street, alone. The New Orleans police force was stretched thin. There just weren't enough good cops. What was he thinking when he took this job? He wished he was someplace safe—like Afghanistan.

His moving flashlight beam caught on pale skin. Someone was crawling onto the embankment.

It was a white guy. Stark naked.

The patrolman called down the slope. "Sir, do you need help?" Dumb question, really. Of course the naked guy needed help.

The crawling man didn't answer. The patrolman reached for his radio to call for assistance.

The whiteness disappeared into blackness under his flashlight beam.

The wolf leapt.

The wolf clamped his jaws on the man's ear and tasted blood.

Cop. This was a cop.

The wolf overpowered the human's mind and paralyzed his consciousness. The wolf became a naked man again. Of all things, that didn't surprise him—his ability to change shape between wolf and man. That felt natural. He'd done that before.

He sucked on the cop's bleeding ear, and knowing rushed into his mind. The manwolf plunged into the patrolman's memories. He found a maelstrom of strange new information. Unbelievable things were mundane in this June day of 2007.

SatelliteInternetInterstateGulf War9/11The Union won the war. HumVeeSuperDomeWho Dat?A hurricane named Katrina.

He broke contact and crawled, a wolf again, slinking through the giant live oak trees, his mind reeling, overfull.

He crouched under the limbs of a half-uprooted weeping willow. Its massive roots jutted up from the ground in a gnarled net of dirt. It was good cover.

He had to wait long for his next quarry. Now he knew what he needed. He needed clothes. But he couldn't enter one of the broken shops or houses. He remembered that the policeman had orders to shoot looters.

He needed a male, built like he was.

While he waited and watched for days on end, amazing things played out before his eyes.

A distant growling drone from above made him peer up through the net of sheltering tree branches. A silver glint slowly arrowed across the sky, drawing a white trail behind it. He knew from the cop's mind that the tiny glint was an airplane. There were people in it.

It was unbelievable. This could not possibly be the same earth he'd been buried in.

Finally his prey presented himself in the early night. The young man was the right height. He was lean. Not as lean as the manwolf was but this man would need to do. Negro wasn't the right word anymore. Black, that was the proper word. The wolf knocked him down from behind, clamped his jaws on his ear, tasted his blood. Another onslaught of new words filled his mind. This was a lawyer at an investment firm.

ATMCredit limitE-bankingE-mailLeverageLatteMarg incallEmployment verificationBarackObamaArmani

The manwolf took the lawyer's clothes. He couldn't make his fingers tie the tie, but that was all right. It was well after happy hour. He knew he could just sling it around his neck and not look out of place.

He took the lawyer's wallet and his watch and his car keys because that's what muggers do. He knew how to run on two legs, even if the shoes were loose.

He knew where the man had parked. The manwolf had made a point of remembering that before he separated from the lawyer's thoughts. He hoped the lawyer wouldn't be willing to run naked through the Vieux Carré to get to his car. But he might just do. The memory lingered that the lawyer owed 50K on his Beemer.

The manwolf found the car. The lawyer was nowhere in sight.

The manwolf pressed the button on the remote key. The driver's side door lock clicked open as the parking lights flashed once.

What now?

After he'd separated from his prey's mind he didn't retain all those details of how to drive. He threw the car keys into a sewer and left on foot.

He sighted a hooker. He knew what she was without someone else's mind to tell him. Some things were timeless. And they were still called hookers. It was strangely comforting to see a prostitute. She would know the sort of things the others hadn't.

AIDSTextingSextingTwitterMethBJBareback

When he let her go she staggered away.

She'd dropped her cell. From her mind he retained how to text but couldn't get his fingers to work those tiny keys even if he had anyone to call. He didn't even know the language well enough to speak it.

Once disconnected, a lot of his new knowledge slipped away. What he managed to keep hold of were things most startling and things most basic. The kind of questions they would ask you if you woke up in the ER.

What is the date?

Who is the President of the United States?

And he knew that they asked you those questions if you were taken to the ER. And he knew the "ER" was

Emergency Room.

It was a different world, this 2007. Blending in was going to be hideously complicated.

Everything was interconnected. Everything was instant. No one waited for anything.

He needed more minds. He needed to know the things that everyone knew before he could pass as one of these digital people.

And then, finally, he could get back to hunting and killing.

Chapter One

March 2012

"Hold on, Lori! Don't do anything! I'll be right there. Please. I need to hang up now. I'm in the car."

Distracted driving laws in Chicago meant you could get stopped for talking hands-free too. Detective John Hamdon was out of his area, behind the wheel, and on the phone. He might not get a break from the local beat cops.

Lori's voice was a piercing wail as he turned off the phone. "You be here! You be here, damn you! Or this is *it!*"

John didn't know what "it" meant exactly. Affair over? He didn't think so. He was almost ready for the affair to end. But he couldn't be the one to break it off. He kept hoping the Lori he used to know would come back.

This it sounded worse than a breakup. He was afraid she meant suicide. And he couldn't count on her to be just twisting him around. Being a cop taught him to never ignore a suicide threat.

He didn't know what happened to her over the last year. The sex? It was never brilliant but there used to be some. Lori was never happy anymore. It made him crazy that he couldn't help her.

He needed to get to her now, right now, but Chicago was no town to get across fast at the best of times. This was Saturday night and the Eisenhower was a parking lot.

John took the back roads. He was on Bellus Road, moving well above the speed limit. A motion drew his glance to his mirror. Darkness flitted across the pavement in his rearview, a motion like a disconnected shadow under a streetlamp. It made him tense up.

It had to be smoke or a swarm of gnats but it just looked *black*. He glanced again. His eyes were off the road only for an instant.

The dog was in front of him, huge in the headlights. John jammed on the brakes with the screech of shredding rubber. He felt a slow motion sensation of the car dragging forward on locked tires. The ass end of the car pulled, trying to kick out to the right. With the sick-making thud of impact, the dog vanished under his car.

Oh shit shit shit. I killed a dog.

No. Not killed. He could hear it under there, feel its thumps, still moving. It wasn't dead yet.

John had a giant wounded animal tearing out his car's muffler.

He was putting his car into park when another impact jumped him forward with a slam from behind. He heard the *whomp* of the airbag deploying as it hit him like a boulder.

Shit!

Dazed, he stared at the blood from his nose dripping onto the air bag. He'd been rear-ended.

Damn. Damn. Damn. God, just hit me again!

Pinned in his seat, he thrashed, desperate to get to Lori. First, he needed to get this fucking airbag out of his way. He jabbed it with his pocket knife. As it deflated he fumbled for his seatbelt latch and door handle at the same time. He spilled out of the car, breathing hard. He let himself go down. One knee hit the pavement, then the other knee.

The car behind his was backing up. John heard the scream of metal parting. He thought the driver was going to hit skip. *God, I didn't mean that literally. I was being sarcastic.* But the other car stopped. John heard it shift into park, its headlights shining forward.

John quickly noted the plate number then put his hands to the asphalt and leaned down to see what was under his own car, afraid of what the dog would look like.

There was no dog.

There was a naked man, young, long, lean and very white in the headlight wash, except for the black hair on his head and the black hair curling thick at his crotch. John took in the vision in an extended instant that could've gone on forever if it was up to him. Dark eyes stared back, wide. John couldn't see their color. Under here, they were just dark. His face was extraordinary, and he was the most beautiful being John had ever seen. One long, exquisitely muscled arm stretched forward. The young man's hand reached toward him.

John blinked.

Like he'd lost a page in a book. He was now looking at a dog.

No, that wasn't a dog, not with that mane, narrow muzzle, and slanted eyes. That was a wolf. It was scrabbling to get its feet under its body, trying to slither out from under the car. Its bushy tail batted John in the face in turning. Its quick-scratching claws sprayed road grit back at him.

A voice sounded behind John, above him—it had to be the man who'd crashed into him from behind—calling him a dipwad.

John backed out from under the car and squinted up at the other driver from a kneeling position. Detective John Hamdon was supposed to be civil and professional at all times, and say sir and ma'am. Instead John asked, "How do you stop when I'm not here?"

"It was a green light!"

The light was a thousand feet up the road.

John touched his nose, then brought away his hand. There was blood on his fingers. Fucking air bag.

The air bag probably saved his life.

He sniffed. He touched his hand to his ear and saw more blood on his fingers. He got to his feet. He put his palm to his chest. It felt bruised.

Flashing lights announced the arrival of a squad car. Well, there was one small break in this shit storm anyway. *You know? Sometimes there really is one of us when you want one.*

The car sounded a single whoop of its siren.

Before the patrolman was even out of his car, the other driver was telling him the light was green. The patrolman was nodding, getting in close enough to smell the guy's breath. It must've been okay, because the patrolman asked the driver if he was hurt, asked for his driver's license, and told him to fill out an accident report.

John was out of his area, so he didn't know the patrolman. The patrolman moved his flashlight beam up and down the blood on John's shirt. "Do you need medical attention, sir?"

"No." He sniffed, swallowed. He tasted the tang of iron in his throat. John gave the patrolman his name, rank, and star number, then pulled out his insurance card and his driver's license. He put out his other hand for the clipboard. "Can I have that?" He wanted to say he was in a hurry. That would be the dead wrong thing to say at an accident scene.

He wrote quickly. He left out his hallucination of a naked man.

The patrolman walked around to the crumpled front

end of his car. He asked John, "Sir? Was there another vehicle involved?"

The beat cop thought John had rear-ended someone else. John shook his head. "I hit a dog."

The patrolman considered the damage. "Big dog," he said like an invitation for John to change his story.

"Tell me about it," John said. Without thinking about it he rubbed the back of his neck.

The other driver called from the shoulder of the road, "Oh, yeah, sure! Why not! Don't start that whiplash act! He caused the accident! He was stopped at a green light. There was no freaking dog. His car was already like that. He's drunk."

The patrolman crossed back to the other driver. As John finished writing his account he heard their voices, the volume going up and up. The other driver was all but screaming. "You're citing *me*? *He* caused the accident!"

The beat cop came back to John to collect his report and return his license.

Pocketing his driver's license, John said wearily, "Please tell me he has insurance. You're gonna tell me he doesn't have insurance."

"Actually, he does. You sure you don't want to go to the ER, Detective?"

"No. I'm fine," John said just before the pavement came up and hit him in the face.

John woke up in the ambulance. They had him in a backboard and cervical collar. The med tech told him he had a broken nose and a broken big toe. He'd probably done the toe himself, mashing on the brake.

Shit shit shit. I gotta see Lori. He tried to get up. He couldn't move at all. They weren't going to let him out of

this rig 'til they nuked his spine. *Oh shit.*
Lori.

It was four o'clock in the morning before the hospital reluctantly discharged him. The X-rays showed no spinal cord damage. The doctor wanted to keep him for observation.

"I need to be somewhere," he said, striding around the offered wheelchair. Under the bright lights of the hospital entrance, he finally thought to ask someone, "Where's my car?"

John tried to call Lori from the taxi. He had no clue what planet his car was on. He'd caught a small break that he hadn't secured his gun inside his car. His service pistol was still in his apartment.

C'mon c'mon c'mon. Lori's phone was off the hook. He tried her cell. It kept rolling over into voicemail.

He had his money ready to pay the cabbie as they pulled up in front of Lori's little yellow bungalow. He left a bigger tip than he wanted, but he wasn't waiting for change. John jumped out of the taxi and charged up the short driveway. He pounded on the door, and jammed the buzzer hard. "Lori!" He jumped into the bushes to look through her bedroom window. He cupped his hands around his eyes to shade out the sunrise glare. Lori wasn't there. Then he saw—oh God almighty—yes, she was there. She was on the floor.

He started back to his car to get a crowbar, then remembered—no car.

He tore off the screen door. He slammed his shoulder at the door with all his strength five times before the door jamb gave way around the deadbolt. He strode inside through black smoke that smelled like nothing. Maybe it wasn't even there. The crash had him a little fucked up. He was *not* going to pass out again.

The bedroom door was locked. He stomp-kicked it in and roared, "*Lori!*"

She lay on her side, her head on a lacy-edged pillow, the corner of a blue woven rug pulled over her like a blanket.

John grabbed the empty pill bottle from the nightstand and pulled the bedside phone down to the floor with him to call 911. He searched for a pulse while he held the receiver between his ear and his shoulder. He kept dropping it. He left the receiver on the floor and rolled Lori onto her back and started mouth to mouth. Between breaths he shouted out the address and signal eight, his name and star number, and the label on the pill bottle. He heard the voice of the dispatcher, sounding very small from the receiver on the floor. She was sending EMS and staying on the line while John did what he needed to do.

He thought he felt a faint pulse. Maybe. Or maybe that was his. His heart was thudding. Lori's lips were cool and bluish.

He felt around on the floor for where he'd left the phone. He picked it up and croaked, "I think I lost her." He could hear sirens, but he couldn't be sure they were his ambulance.

Then he saw it. On the bed. There was a note. He knelt up and grabbed it. Something turned in his stomach as he read on pink-flowered paper: *John, why did you let me die?* He wanted to trash that note. He shouldn't have touched it. He let it drop.

He got back on his knees, trying to get Lori to breathe.

John slumped in the armchair in front of the TV. He didn't turn it on. He was on indefinite leave pending an investigation by Internal Affairs. The investigation was taking two times forever. Days and nights oozed together. How long had he been off duty now? A week? Two? And there was no promise of his returning—ever. IA saw dirt everywhere they looked. John had used a phone at the scene to call 911. He'd contaminated the scene by moving the suicide note. He'd failed to give assistance to a suicidal woman. He'd deliberately caused a traffic accident to give himself time to let a woman he was tired of die. What had he really hit with his car? The other driver hadn't seen a dog. Where was the carcass? Did he and the deceased own any property in common? John Hamdon had a thirty-five thousand dollar lump sum deposit in a bank account in Cleveland he hadn't reported to the IRS six years ago. Did the detective want to tell Internal Affairs what that was for?

At that John had stood up. "We're done." And he'd walked out of the interview.

No one from the department had contacted him since then.

He didn't know what time it was. The only light was from the cold fluorescents in the kitchen. He couldn't even mourn Lori. He would need to do that later. The only thing he felt toward her right now was anger. The note really tore it. *John, why did you let me die?*

Right. Put it on me, sweetheart. God damn it, I did everything I could. Are you happy now?

He stared at that guy reflected in the dark screen, surprised he didn't look worse. It was the hair that gave the illusion of him having it all together. He kept his hair short, mowed flat on the top. Hair that short can't turn on you. He was tall and well built, but that guy slouching in the TV screen was not what he wanted to see.

I didn't mean that, Lori. I'm sorry.

He thought of the naked young man under his car. Where had that hallucination come from? John couldn't make up anyone like that. But obviously he had.

He got up, changed into sweats, and jogged down three flights of stairs. His apartment building was an old brownstone, not in the best neighborhood. He ran around several blocks—some of them unlit—almost hoping to get jumped so he could let loose on some jackass, but John Hamdon just didn't look like anyone to fuck with, and no one did.

John stood before the Chicago Police Department Headquarters, a great slab of a building rising five stories high, but it looked squat because it spread across a full city block. A perimeter of stubby anti-ram bollards out by the sidewalks made the place look like a fortress. Because of the Internal Affairs investigation, John had been out longer this time than when he'd been shot three years ago. After a solid month, he felt like a stranger here.

He jogged up the stairs to the fourth floor. The first person John saw in the Central Investigations Section offices was the last person he wanted to see—Detective Chuck Wallice.

Chuck Wallice was a total bastard—the guy who became a cop because he liked to brandish a gun and tell people what to do. He only left Patrol for the money. Chuck looked like a poster man for Law Enforcement, with broad shoulders, Superman jaw, cheekbones like armor plating, craterous dimples, steroidal muscles, and a build like a plastic mannequin. Another thing Chuck had in common with the plastic men in the store window—no discernable nuts. That explained why, as much as Chucky talked about sex, he never showed wood. John was not sure how Chuck was passing the physical.

On seeing John returned after a month's absence, Chuck Wallice was his usual sensitive self. "Hamdon. What are you doing here?"

"Me? I'm just here for the donuts." John walked past him.

John was aware of heads leaning out from office doors—lots of eyes. Admins and detectives turned around in their chairs. Some of them stood up. Their murmurs of welcome back made him feel good.

Detective Thea Pittman-Jones stepped out of her office. Thea was tall and black—not as black as Antwan Ramadan, who was standing behind her—but no one was blacker than Antwan. Thea was a former Olympic biathlete. She wasn't much for hugging anyone other than her man and her two kids, but she gave John a warm one. "I didn't get to tell you, John, I'm sorry for your loss."

"Thank you," he said quietly.

Detective Antwan Ramadan stepped out from behind Thea. The only thing white on Antwan was his teeth. Not even the whites of his eyes were white. He had no fat on him. None. His muscles were distinct blocks. He was built wide across the shoulders, narrow at the hips. It wasn't even a carrot shape. Antwan was a wedge. He was a good half foot shorter than Thea and John. Antwan gave John a light fist tap on the biceps instead of a hug. "Yeah. Wasn't your fault. You know that. You know her history better than anyone."

"I shouldn't have gone there," John said. "I should have sent EMS. I screwed up. It cost Lori her life."

Thea's long forefinger poked his way. "Don't go there, John. You do not go there. You hear what I'm telling you? That woman has a list of 911 calls as long as my arm." Thea had long arms. "You just got hit for the one threat she went through with."

John didn't want to think too long about Lori. The pit was waiting for him there. He asked, "What'd Forensics find on my car?" *Like—I don't know—maybe a naked young man hung up in my undercarriage?*

"They couldn't identify the fur and the hair on your muffler," Antwan said. "Coulda been something your tires spun up from the road for all anyone knows. Lab says you did *not* hit a person, and you did *not* hit another car."

"Told 'em so," John muttered.

Antwan said, "They can't even tell *what* you hit, but you laid down a buncha feet of road crayon trying to stop for something. The guy behind you? Not so much."

Thea held up a circled fingers-and-thumb zero.

"Good. He can fix my car," John said.

He walked the rest of the welcoming gauntlet toward the commander's office.

When John knocked on the door jamb of Commander Scott's office, the gray eyes looked up, but the head stayed face toward the desk so the commander looked like a charging rhino. "You all here, Hamdon?"

"Yes, sir."

Commander Scott was a big square rock of a former Marine. He still had the haircut, buzzed much, much closer than John's. The commander was old school, not much for showing or talking about emotion.

The commander pushed John's gun and star across the desktop. He'd had them out, waiting for him. "Get back in the ring."

John overheard someone in one of the administrative offices talking about "the new guy."

John was surprised. Turnover was low in the Central Investigations Section. He asked the first person he met in the hallway. "We have a new guy?"

"His name's Bast," Detective Marvin Meyers said, tossing his pen up in the air so that it turned a triple flip. He caught it again. "He's from New Orleans, so you know what they call him."

"Bastard," John said.

"No. They call him N'Orleans, dick." It sounded like *Norlins* the way Meyers said it.

John sensed someone standing close behind him. He turned around to face a young man, a striking son of a bitch, who said in a surprisingly low Cajun drawl, "Hi, I'm N'Orleans Dick."

John crossed his arms, looked him up and down. "I'm Cleveland Asshole. I think we've met."

"I'm sure we haven't," Bast said, but his half-shut eyes and the near smile said something else entirely. In fact, that face said they'd had sex.

Bast was the kind of being who walks into a room and everyone else turns into wallpaper. Beige wallpaper. His hair was thick and dark with a slight wave to it, his eyes so dark they were nearly black, his skin pale—not sickly pale. It was more a smooth ivory white. He was built slender, kind of feral, and he was real tall when not curled up naked under a Chevy, maybe even taller than John was, but he had a lazy slouchy way of standing. He was an amazing presence. And way too familiar.

John knew that face, the upswept features, the high cheekbones crowding his eyes. John had seen that face under his car. And that tousled shock of dark hair—the one on his head—that was the same. John couldn't see the other thatch of dark hair now. Bast was wearing black denim trousers. He was perfectly incredible. John was not likely to forget him. And Bast shouldn't be able to forget

John either. "Are you sure I didn't run you over?"

"Did I enjoy it, *cher*?" Bast asked airily. "Because I don't think I would."

The brush-off got John pissed. *I saw you*. That was the face. Why didn't Bast admit it? Okay, John knew damn well why Bast didn't admit it. Because it didn't happen. Bast's couldn't be the face John had seen underneath a car by headlamp light at night a little before John passed out. This must be one of those created memories that shrinks talked about.

But this guy had the same preternatural beauty that John thought he remembered. In the glare of office light he could see more details. Bast had a beguiling, pretty mouth and a strong, masculine jaw line. His ears were set close to his head and angled off at the top, suggesting animal ears. There was an exotic hint of a slant to his dark eyes.

Commander Scott appeared from his office to introduce them, "Bast, this is Detective John Hamdon."

John freed up his right hand to offer it to Bast. "Does Bast got a first name?"

Bast grasped John's hand in a firm grip with long, elegant fingers. "René," said Bast.

The commander said, "Detective Bast will be taking over for Andy."

John did a double take. *Detective* Bast? John had thought the new guy was a civilian member of the department.

John waited until Marv Meyers took Bast on the rest of the tour of the fourth floor to ask the commander, "What happened to the one-year residency requirement before you can test—no exceptions?"

When John first came to Chicago six years ago he had been bucked back down to beat cop. He had to wait a year until he could take the detective test. So this guy rolled into town and jumped over everyone who was actually qualified, did he?

The commander said, "*Apparently* someone upstairs thinks honorable service in post-Katrina New Orleans counts like a tour in Baghdad." He meant upstairs literally. The honchos were on the fifth floor. He paused to give his head a slight side tilt and opened his hands as if to say *Whatever*. "They let him test. But he still had to score better than all the Chicago officers taking the exam."

"He didn't," John said. But obviously Bast had.

The commander's stone face looked baffled. "He nailed it."

John looked into Detective Bast's office. It used to be Z's office. Andy Zupancic had retired. Solid man, Z. John didn't like seeing someone else's stuff in there.

Detective Georgia Grover came up behind him in the doorway. She got on tiptoe and still couldn't see over John's shoulder. "Whatcha see?"

John turned and jerked his thumb back at the new guy's office. "Z had a picture of Albert Einstein up there."

Georgia nodded. "Yeah. I always thought that was kind of weird and interesting about Z."

Andy was a blue-collar, beer-drinking, bowling league guy. You just didn't expect the cerebral Einstein up there. Poker playing dogs, yeah. Einstein, not really.

John said, "Guess what this jackstand has hanging there."

"No idea."

"Guess. Just guess."

"I don't know." Georgia tossed up her little hands. "Fluffy bunnies."

"A mirror," John said. He stood aside for Georgia to see in.

"A big one," Georgia said, leaning in the doorway. "Guess he's always got one eye in the mirror."

"I'm exceptionally good looking," Bast spoke from behind them.

Georgia turned scarlet.

Bast continued languidly, "Red is not a good color on you, *cher*."

John was afraid Bast was right. Not about Georgia in red. Bast really was exceptionally good looking.

His lush, non-regulation mane of dark hair was just *that* much too long. It was on his collar and it brushed his ears. It had a slight wave and it was too sexy for a police department. A man's hair was not supposed to cover his ears at all. John found it distracting. Not just the hair. Bast had a way of being. He was a sexual presence that could make a man think about switch hitting. Bast was smoking hot. Bast was all wrong.

The commander slow-marched up the hall and handed papers to Bast. "You need to report for the two-day orientation training. It's mandatory for all nonsupervisory sworn members assigned to a field unit with citizen-dress responsibilities in the Detective Division."

Meyers spoke aside to Bast. "They'll teach you how to wear clothes."

"That's why I wanted this job, *cher*," Bast said. "I just don't look good in blue."

The commander told him, "See Paul Drake. He's the Assistant Deputy Superintendent, Education and Training Division."

"Yes, sir." Bast turned down the hall. John caught himself watching his retreating ass. A lot of motion in his rolling walk, not a woman's side to side rock, but those narrow hips and tight ass were into it.

The commander called after him, "Oh, and N'Orleans!"

Bast turned.

"Get a haircut!"

John woke up coming. This was no sleep-through-it wet dream. This was an eye-crossing, ball-clenching full jack, and he cried out loud. He lay back, catching his breath, fists closed on bunched sheets. Memory of dark eyes and velvet lashes lingered, with the sensation of hot tongue and full lips on his cock. He'd felt and seen everything vividly. Vivid enough for him to get up, turn on all the lights, and search his efficiency apartment. Everything was undisturbed, except for him. He didn't smell anything unexpected on the bed. He would have noticed. Bast had a distinct scent, strong, male, and thrilling.

John returned to bed, assured that he was alone. And a little disappointed.

Chapter Two

Before roll call, during the last dash to the break room for coffee, Bast appeared, back from Orientation, his hair smartly cut, his gray sport coat and charcoal trousers properly conservative, his tie something a Republican would wear. He still didn't look like a cop. And he was still too damn sexy.

"Glad that's over. I don't care for Drake," Bast said off-handedly. "He has a mustache."

"A mustache?" John blurted. "That's it? That's what's off-putting? A mustache?"

"This is a surprise to you, *cher*?"

"I'm thinking something else. Like, oh, I don't know, like a penis."

"I could always figure out something to do with that."

In the CIS conference room Detective René Bast surveyed the mountain range of piled folders that was the Krieg case. There were also hundreds more data files on thumb drives, CDs, and ancient microfiches. The cartel boss had a long criminal history.

And they don't know the half of it.

The section was working through lunch to go over the files. An admin ordered in pizza. The drug lord was named Krieg. That was it. Just Krieg. He was a citizen of Uruguay. His grandfather had emigrated from Germany in 1945. Krieg's organization had tentacles up and through

Central America all the way north to Chicago. The FBI was on the interstate drug trafficking part of the case. Chicago PD was on it because Krieg currently resided in Chicago.

And René Bast was here because of Krieg.

Detective Georgia Grover came to stand alongside Bast and stare at the piles. "Paper-free society, huh?" Georgia said.

Bast gave a *hmm* of agreement. Of the detectives in the Central Intelligence Section, Georgia was the nice one, Antwan Ramadan the easy one, Thea Pittman-Jones the professional one. The commander was an old veteran, as exciting as a pair of brown socks. Detective Meyers was in the wiseguy slot. Meyers was the ranking detective in the section. He was a lieutenant. Chuck Wallice held down the asshole position—every unit had one. Then there was John Hamdon. What to make of this *bougre*?

John Hamdon was muscular. Not like Wallice, who was a bad joke. Hamdon was the guy Wallice was trying to be and failing miserably.

John Hamdon had a squared jaw, firm chin, no dimple. His mouth could be fuller, but it had a determined look, only slightly softer at the corners. His narrow eyes glinted pale brown. They looked hard under the fluorescent lights. They were eyes of a tough hombre. There was no preening about him. He was pure, raw male.

Bast liked men taller than he was. John was a frog's hair under Bast's six-foot-one. For someone like John, Bast could deal.

A scar across John's straight, sharply chiseled nose made him look like a battered movie hero, or the villain. He didn't wear a wedding band, and there was no picture of a woman on his desk, but there was a snapshot of a grinning little boy who looked like John, only cute. John wasn't cute.

He was obviously gay—obvious to Bast anyway—and in the closet. Bast despised closet-dwellers. And there Hamdon was, all buff and butch, all alpha, and he didn't have the balls to step out.

And he hates me. Why?

Bast knew that John had seen him for a split-instant in the dark under his car. John shouldn't be able to believe what he saw. What he saw was completely incredible, and John had to know he'd been pretty banged up when he saw it. Why wasn't he letting it go?

John Hamdon must have that extra sense, like some animals have, to know when someone is not what he appears to be. That made him dangerous.

Bast needed to read him. He needed an opening to get into John Hamdon's head.

And there it is.

Marv Meyers was ducking into his office. Meyers had scratches on the backs of both hands—new kitty from the look of them. That was half the battle right there. But Bast couldn't exactly lick Meyers' hands. Blood-to-blood was the only other choice. Bast would have him only for a moment. *Make it count.* Bast made a shallow cut in his own palm with his pocket knife, then breezed into Meyers' office. He reached across Meyers' desk as if to snag a pen for a minute, but knocked over Meyers' phone charger. As Meyers reached to set it right, Bast reached too, and accidentally-on-purpose grabbed Meyers' hand instead of the phone. Palm-cut pressed to cat scratches. Bast got into Meyers for an instant. It was enough.

"Sorry," Bast said, letting go. The cut in his palm was already closing up. He picked up the pen.

"Klutz," said Meyers, replacing his phone in its charger.

"Mary Murphy," Bast said.

Meyers' eyes went as round as human eyes could round.

"First crush," Bast said.

Marv sputtered. "I never told *anyone* that. I never even told *Mary!* How—?"

"Lucky guess," Bast said.

It had the intended effect. As soon as Meyers returned to the conference room he reported to all the detectives there, "Everybody watch out for N'Orleans. He's a mind reader."

"Oh yeah?" Chuck called across the room, "Hey, Bast! Read my mind!"

Bast answered coolly without looking at him. "Assumes a fact not in evidence."

"Huh?"

"That's lawyer-speak," John said.

Apparently John Hamdon had been in enough courtrooms to know what Bast really said. Chuck's question assumed that Chuck had a mind to be read.

Antwan Ramadan picked up the dare. "Read a mind, Bast. Go on. But not mine."

Bast surveyed the room. He didn't want to go straight for his real target. He chose Georgia Grover. Georgia was in her late forties, decidedly blonde, with a matronly build. Georgia wore as much makeup as the directive allowed. She was sweet and sympathetic. Witnesses talked to her. Georgia had paper cuts on her right hand.

Bast gave her a smile and crooked his forefinger at her to come. She blushed, put down her pizza, cleaned her hands, and circled the table to him, while, under the table, Bast sliced his palm again with the straight edge of a piece of paper.

As Georgia presented herself to be read, Bast stood up and took her hand. She winced, looked blank for a moment, then apologized for her flinch. "Stings. Paper cut."

Bast took her other hand, the one not cut. He already

had what he wanted. "You had an imaginary friend when you were little."

Chuck made a raspberry. "Oh, like any girl doesn't."

Bast said, "It was a ghost. His name was Roger."

Georgia's eyes went wide. They were gray. "No way!"

Count on John Hamdon to say, "You talked to her mother, didn't you, Bast?"

Bast continued. "You had five wooden mice. Red, blue, green, yellow and violet. They were part of a game. You never played the game. You just liked the mice. The red one was your favorite."

Georgia got flustered, and waved her free hand. "Oh my God! Oh my God! Oh my God. Stop!"

Bast kissed her hand before he let it go.

Marv Meyers asked, "How often does that happen, Bast? You get asked to stop?"

"More times than I'd like." And with a side wink to John he added, "I think I'd rather be run over."

John's face darkened.

Bast smiled at him. *Catch me if you can, Cleveland Asshole.*

John wasn't hard on the eyes. No, that wasn't true. John was painful to look at. Just how hard could a cock get? But at the end of the day John Hamdon was just another mayfly. Whatever John thought he knew wasn't getting him anywhere.

You are so far out of your league.

Thea Pittman-Jones leaned over to Georgia. "Was he right, George?"

Georgia was the color of a fire engine—a Chicago fire engine, not one of those lime-colored things other cities used. "Well, *yeah!*"

Antwan Ramadan pointed his pen Bast's way. "There's that Louisiana hoodoo. That's what that is."

"It's called swamp gas," John said.

Georgia asked Bast, "How'd you do it? Are you some kind of mentalist?"

"No," Bast said. "Just mental."

"I was going to say that if you didn't." John Hamdon was leaning against the wall, a fine-looking stud with his arms crossed. He must've realized he was in a defensive posture because he loosened his arms and stepped forward. "Do me."

Bast struggled not to smile. *You are too easy, cher!* "With pleasure."

"I didn't say it like that. And don't try to say I was thinking it."

"I can't say that. I'm not reading you yet." Bast rounded the table.

Bast's paper cut had already healed. He needed an open wound. As he brushed by the wall map, he covertly snagged a pushpin. He pressed the point into his palm, drawing blood. Then, passing behind Antwan's chair, he let the pushpin slip from his hand, unseen, to the floor.

Bast knew that John routinely worked out in a gym before roll call. It looked like Hamdon had been hammering the crap out of a weight bag this morning. He'd knocked some of the bark off his knuckles. The scrapes on his left hand were not completely closed.

"I need your hand."

John offered his right hand.

"Left hand," Bast said.

John shrugged. "Your game." He put out his left hand.

Now Bast would get to see what made John run.

Run, John, run.

Bast took John's hand. It was rough, broad, warm, and manly.

Bast didn't know what his own face looked like.

"Well?" John's voice startled him. Bast hadn't felt him about to speak. "Are we going steady?"

"You're a brick," Bast said, letting go his hand, unsettled. "I got nothing."

"You can't read my mind. What a shock."

"It *is* a shock," Bast said honestly. It was disturbing. He tried not to show how shaken he was. He'd made the connection—blood to blood—and got nothing.

Thea swiveled her chair around, her brown eyes directed up at Bast. "I still want to know how you did what you did with George."

Bast inwardly blessed her for the diversion.

Meyers said, "Yeah, Sherlock. How'd you do that?"

John took his seat and leaned into Georgia Grover, nudging her with his shoulder. "Yeah. How long did you two rehearse that routine, George?"

Georgia looked confused, then seemed to realize what John was insinuating. "You mean—Oh! No! I—"

John said, "You're a good actress."

"I'm not acting!" Georgia said. "René really read my mind somehow."

"Uh huh," John said, dryly. "I still love you, George."

"Interesting," Bast said, watching John warily. "Everyone else is trying to figure out how I did it and you're figuring out how I *didn't*."

John said, "You admit you didn't."

Bast felt his brows contract. "No. I just said it's interesting how you think."

John was supposed to be going over his share of the data mountain that was the Krieg case. Instead of concentrating, he was thinking about Bast. The touch of that man's hand holding his had sent him into orbit. Bast's smooth warmth and masculine scent aroused him. His touch had only been for only a moment, and John still felt the lingering sensation of Bast's skin against his, his own exhilaration, and a deep-seated fear. He pushed that part out of his head. He had no reason to fear this guy. After you've been shot, not a lot scares you.

John had been uneasy when Bast first lowered his brow in an expression of concentration for his mind-reading stunt. If Bast had come up with anything true and painful, John would've known this faker had been in his personnel file. *And I'd'a killed him.* John had a lot of shit behind him that he didn't want in the air.

A touch on the back of his hand brought him back to here and now. "Yo, Cleveland." It was Georgia, leaning across the conference table, tapping him with the side of her pen.

John looked up from the file. "What?"

"You're grinding your teeth."

John consciously relaxed his jaw. It ached. He guessed he'd been grinding.

"What up?" Georgia asked. "Whatcher problem?"

John looked around to see where Bast was. Bast had gone out and hadn't come back yet. John leaned forward, so he and Georgia were shielded between manila stacks of Krieg files. "Bast," John said, very low. "He's wrong."

"About what?"

"No. I mean *he* is *wrong*. He's dirty."

Georgia hunched in closer and whispered urgently, "What do you know?"

"Nothing. But everything in me says he's got to be taken down. I don't like him. I don't like his attitude. I don't like how he talks. He's got that mush mouth thing happening."

"Really?" Georgia sat back, cheerful again. "I think the way Bast talks sounds kind of soft and easy and sexy."

Thea, seated beside John, said without turning, "I do too."

Actually, Bast's voice did sound all that. He had a soft,

rolling, muddy, lazy way of talking. His th's sounded like d's. And he said *don't* instead of *doesn't*. That should've made him sound ignorant. Instead he sounded laid-back and seductive. But Bast was not some po' boy from down in da swamp and John was not going to be suckered in by a soft and low way of talking. He said, "Thea, you just like him 'cause he can't say the word 'ask.'"

Bast couldn't put the s and k sounds together. He said *ax* instead of *ask*.

John got a punch in the arm from Thea for that, kind of hard.

"And he has that hair. Those eyes," Georgia said dreamily.

"He's tall," Thea added. "You have to admit he's handsome."

"No," John said. The son of a bitch was slightly on the gorgeous side. But John didn't have to admit it.

Thea crisply set down her pen and faced John. "You just don't like him because he's gay."

"That's not it at all," John promised her. "I don't care if he does it with bagels as long as the bagels consent."

Chuck, whose ears were tuned to the gossip channel, was suddenly standing over their end of the conference table. "Who's gay?"

"Bast," Georgia said.

"No," Chuck said in disbelief.

"Yeah." Thea sang the word in two notes. "He's not exactly in the closet."

"If he was any farther out of it, he'd be in the parking lot," John said.

Thea asked, "You have a problem with that, Cleveland?"

"No," John said. *Actually yes. I don't like him looking that good when I know he's all wrong.* "Just saying."

Chuck's thin mouth tightened into a smirk. "There's

got to be a line in here about a Cajun Queen."

Thea's voice was a warning kind of quiet. "No, Chuck, there doesn't."

John got up. He was allergic to Chuck. This looked like a good time to get a coffee refill.

He found Bast in the break room, looking off-pissing smug. At least Bast wasn't repellant like Chuck was. Bast was too attractive. He'd just taken a sip of hot coffee and his lips were red. John could imagine where he could put those lips.

"There you are, *cher*."

"Don't call me *cher*." *Where else would I be, Bast?* "I'm not your *cher*."

"I threaten you."

John sputtered. "You are such a dick."

"It's why you love me."

"Who ever said I love you?"

"You. In so many ways."

"You're fucking with my head."

"Not in the office, *cher*. Maybe after work."

Yes, the head was definitely fucked. How could Bast know which side of the plate John swung from, when John only three-quarters knew it and didn't really admit it? *I'm not in the closet. It's just dark in here and there are shoes.*

The wolf prowled along the high, quarry-stone wall, agitated. The night was dry and warm. The feeling of unease was getting stronger. Then his head was exploding. Hatred swelled inside him. He paced back and forth in front of the wall, quick turn by quick turn, his tail twitching. Then he was trotting, his mane standing up.

It was in there.

The wolf dug.

He slithered under the wall, then shook dirt off his coat in the park-like woods. He crept toward the lights. They were soft and low, like twilight, only bright enough for a man to find his way.

Near the great house the woods opened up. There was a built-in kidney-shaped pool. Shifting planes of the water reflected the light of a full moon. An inflated blue mattress floated in the pool, a man asleep upon it. The wolf smelled the man through the miasma of chlorine. The man smelled of mosquito repellent and something much, much stronger.

The wolf's hackles were raised up stiff. Overhead, the full moon shone bright. The wolf was sick under its goad.

The wolf would have one chance. It would be a disaster if he missed.

He waited behind the row of tall ornamental grasses. Their white feathery heads nodded in the slight breeze.

Eventually the mattress floated closer. The wolf crept out from his cover, and stalked closer, belly to the ground, his ears hard forward. He made no sound. He would have only one chance.

A bird woke with a startled cry. The man stirred.

The wolf leapt.

Roll Call. 5 June 2012. 0800 Hours.

John, who was used to getting up early and going to the gym, barely got to headquarters in time for roll call. He nursed a cup of strong coffee in the back row, trying to wake up. His eyes kept shutting, and he nodded over his coffee cup. He remembered letting his little boy take a taste of his coffee once. John had ended up wearing that.

He told Daniel he would probably like it better when he was older.

At the front of the room, the commander stood up to get updates on the detectives' current cases, and to assign new cases. "New case," the commander announced. "Our dear friend Manolo was found with his throat ripped out, most likely by a large dog."

That woke John up. There was a rustling through the room.

"Dead?" Chuck asked.

Meyers leaned over to Chuck. "Did the commander mention he had his throat ripped out?"

"Who?" Georgia said. It looked like Chuck wasn't the only one having a hard time believing good news. "Manolo? Manolo is dead? Really?"

"Oh, weeping and gnashing of teeth," Thea Pittman-Jones said.

"All broke up, aren't you, Pitt?" Antwan said.

"I'd sing hallelujah, but laughing over the dead's just not right."

"I'll laugh," Chuck said.

Bast sneezed, *tchu*.

The commander spoke over them. "We will not underplay this case just because we're all happy with the outcome."

"But I loved him," Georgia said, straight-faced.

The commander shut his eyes. His mouth became a thin line for a moment. "Okay. I get it. Hoorah." He opened his eyes. In a voice that said *we will cut the crap right now*, the commander went on. "Now. There is a possibility that it was a hit. Manolo doesn't have a dog. Dogs don't normally hunt down cartel bosses who deserve to die. We need to find the dog and the dog's handler."

"Why isn't the Organized Crime Division doing this?" Meyers said with a wave at the firewall. OCD offices were on the other side.

"Dead-by-dog isn't any cartel's MO," the commander said. "This incident might not have anything to do with gang activities."

"Did the coroner get a dental impression on the bite?" Georgia asked.

"No, because Manolo looks like this."

The commander projected a PowerPoint slide up onto a blank wall. There was a collective *oh* from just about all of them. The commander had been strictly literal about that throat-ripped-out thing. No one was getting a dental impression from that. That was a rip.

John glanced around at his section. Chuck was leaning forward, intent. *Try not to drool, boy.* Bast kept a steady gaze, his face like a beautiful statue. Thea, Antwan, and Meyers all wore grimaces and narrowed eyes as if to limit how much of the grisly image they could take in. Georgia looked at the floor.

"Coroner puts the cause of death as asphyxiation."

John puzzled over that one. *So he was dead before the throat came out?*

"Why isn't there more blood?" Antwan asked.

"He was in the pool. He bled out in the pool."

"Chlorine. A murderer's best friend," Meyers said.

"And his bodyguards hauled him out before EMS got there," the commander added. "He was thoroughly dead before then. Crime Scene questioned the bodyguards. See Forensics. They may have found this killer animal on the security camera recordings from Manolo's mansion for that night."

"Doesn't a dog get one bite?" Georgia asked.

"This was one fatal bite. Game over. And we don't *know* that this was his first bite."

"It offed Manolo," Chuck said. "Can't we give the mutt a medal?"

"Don't go there. Any of you. There is no such thing as a righteous hit."

Bast said, "Then you *do* think it's a hit, Commander."

"Men like Manolo don't just randomly meet gruesome ends," the commander said. And probably because Bast was the only one not singing *Ding Dong Manolo's Dead,* he said, "Bast, it's your case. Liaise with OCD."

John leaned forward and murmured to Bast, "That's Organized Crime Division, not obsessive compulsive disorder."

Bast turned in his seat. "OCD?" he whispered back, assuming a clueless look. He batted thick eyelashes at John. "Spell it."

Just as the commander added, "And Bast. Take Cleveland with you."

Bast drove the plain brown police sedan out to Manolo's property. John Hamdon rode in the passenger seat, not talking. Bast met him silence for silence.

It was like John knew something. But that wasn't possible.

Bast steered the car in through the high iron gates out of Chicago and into instant Miami. The colors inside Manolo's high-walled oasis of wealth were turquoise, coral, and sunshine. Bast opened the driver's side door to baking swelter.

All detectives had to keep their ties and jackets on in public, with their IDs clipped outboard of their clothes in plain sight. It was too hot for this, even though Bast was more used to it than John. They were both dressed in regulation boring: Bast in shades of blue-gray, John in tans.

The first responders and the pool filters had made hash of the scene within the yellow tape. The pool itself was clear.

"Who turned the filters back on?" John asked.

"According to the preliminary report, Crime Scene turned them off."

No one answered him.

Bast suggested cautiously, "You're thinking this was an inside job and cover-up?"

"No." John sounded annoyed. "I'm thinking that Señora Manolo didn't like the look of that nasty blood in her pool."

"Cameras," Bast said, keeping his voice neutral. "They're focused on all the house entrances, the roof, and the perimeter walls of the grounds."

John flipped through pages of the preliminary report. "Review of the camera recordings indicates that nothing came in or out of the house, through the front gate, or over the perimeter wall last night."

"There aren't any cameras on the pool," Bast said. "Are there supposed to be?"

"Mister Manolo likes his privacy," said the guard who had attached himself to Bast.

John read aloud from the preliminary report. "Witnesses said Manolo was fond of sleeping on an inflatable mattress in the pool when the weather allowed. The mattress was found still intact, still floating." He looked up from the report. "Where is it?"

"Your people took it," his guard said.

Bast said, "You're right, John. We're not going to find anything here. Let's go review what Forensics came up with." He started back toward the car, expecting John to fall in step.

John said, "I'm taking a walk." And he set off in the other direction, into the woods. Bast had no choice but to follow.

Two bodyguards stuck to John and Bast like shadows.

"Nothing came *over* the wall," John said, tramping through brush along the high perimeter wall. "We know that. The dog didn't come in the gate. We know that. Forensics found no signs of dog at all on the grounds, which means the dog doesn't live here. We know that. Means the hound of the Baskervilles came and went *under* the wall."

Bast's voice sounded behind him. "Crime Scene did a walk of the perimeter."

"I think that's hunky dory," John said. And he only found the hole under the wall because he knew there had to be one, and he wasn't leaving without finding it.

The hole was at the back of the property, near an outlet for rainwater, where the footers weren't so deep. It had been filled back in with loose dirt. In Crime Scene's defense, the hole was really hard to spot.

In Bast's defense—No. There was no defending Bast. It was like Bast didn't want to find this hole.

John noted the GPS coordinates on his handheld, then looked around for security cameras. "That camera." He pointed. "What's the ID of that one? I want to see that recording. And that one." He pointed several yards over and on the other side of the wall.

"It's pointing a little high," Bast said.

"Then maybe we'll catch the tip of an ear," John said, irritated. Bast wasn't a hell of a lot of help on this investigation for being the lead.

John flipped open his phone and called Forensics. He requested the recordings from the two security cameras for the night of the killing. Then he red-taped off the area around the hole on both sides of the wall to reserve it for Crime Scene to process.

Roll Call. 7 June 2012. 0800 hours.

The commander called for case statuses. "Bast! Cleveland! The Manolo case."

That met with a baseline muttering of "bow wow woof woof." The commander lifted a stout finger for silence.

Bast gave the report. "We still don't have an accurate description of the dog. It never crossed line of sight of a security camera. Evidence suggests the dog may have dug a hole to gain access to the grounds and left the way it came."

He played the first video from the camera that monitored outside the wall.

The image was dark. The security light was not helping; it was making the shadows darker. Everyone leaned forward, squinting. John sat in the back with his arms crossed.

Bast pointed at the projection on the wall. "You won't be able to see the hole or the animal, but right here at the bottom you can just see what looks like dirt flying up."

Arcs of dark specks and clods flew fast and furious from the lower edge of the picture.

"Is that a dog or a backhoe?" Meyers said.

Bast then played the video from the security camera trained on the wall from the inside.

"This is possible evidence of the dog leaving the scene twenty minutes later." The leafy top of a small sapling in the foreground abruptly bent over and out of the picture, then sprang back up as if it had been walked over on the ground below the camera's focus.

"If these images show the dog coming and going, that would put the victim's time of death at oh three hundred hours, which jives with the Coroner's estimated time of death."

"Good job, N'Orleans!" Antwan gave Bast a slow

clap. "Good eyes!" He sounded impressed.

Bast left out the fact that it was John who found the hole and had done all the requesting and reviewing of the camera recordings. Bast had overlooked everything he could possibly overlook. John bit his lips.

Bast was adding to his report that the hole had been filled in from the outside—another thing John had noticed that Bast had tried to miss.

"In and out," Meyers said, amazed. "That's not a dog, that's a guided missile."

"And it covered its tracks." The commander rose, menacing. He seemed to grow in size. "*That* is a hit."

Bast nodded.

"Bounce the case back to Organized Crime," the commander ordered.

Thea raised her hand. "But assassination by dog? That doesn't fit any gang's profile."

"Not the weapon I'd use," Chucky said.

"That's because we're not supposed to assassinate people, Chuck," Bast said.

"Can we get a pass for the dog?" Georgia said. "It's a bright, trainable animal and someone made him into a killer."

The commander bellowed, "Do not humanize or make a hero out of this killer. It's not like the dog knew its victim was a drug dealing monster!"

Chapter Three

John let himself into Bast's office, planted his hands on Bast's desk, and asked point blank, "Who are you working for?"

"Uhm." Bast put on a thoughtful face for a moment, then ventured a guess. "City of Chicago?"

"You don't have a birth record."

"Ever hear of a little breeze called Katrina?" Bast asked back, his sexy eyes all innocence.

"Yeah. That's a giant get out of jail free card right there. All the places you supposedly worked lost their records during Katrina. Your original set of fingerprints? Katrina. Your high school? Katrina. Anything earlier than a couple years back, your past just got blown completely away."

Bast lounged back in his chair. Beautiful son of a bitch was almost smiling. No, that was an outright smile. "You know? You're a real good dick, John."

"I don't know who you're working for but it's not Chicago. You're going down."

"Right back at you, *cher*."

That jerked John back upright. He wasn't ready for a counter attack. He didn't have anything illegal to hide, but Bast's threat surprised him.

At least John now knew for certain there was something in Bast's background that Bast didn't want him to see.

Bast didn't know why John Hamdon was snapping at him like a wounded animal. More than ever, Bast needed to know John Hamdon. It still bothered Bast that he'd hit a brick wall instead of John's memories when he'd touched his blood. Bast needed to know John's past, and take him down before John found something on him first.

John had a past. Anyone could see that. He'd left Cleveland for some reason. He'd taken a big pay cut and a demotion to do it. Why?

What are you running from? What's your big secret?

From office chatter Bast knew that John had an ex-wife back in Cleveland. So on the weekend, Bast hopped a cheap stand-by flight out of Midway to Cleveland and tracked her down.

The former Mrs. John Hamdon was a blue-eyed blonde, beautiful in a superficial way. Bast introduced himself as an IRS official looking for John Hamdon. "Is he in trouble?" Vanessa asked, sounding hopeful. "I'll tell you anything I know."

She was easily charmed, so Bast could touch her. She had a bee sting on the back of her lovely neck. Bast hoped it was enough to let him in. He pricked the heel of his hand on the thorn of a pink rose in Vanessa's garden, and he laid his palm on her nape.

Immediately he felt like he'd dived head first into a shallow pool. Under Vanessa's perfect, polished surface, Bast hit hard disappointment, anger, blame, betrayal, pain, and a hole in her soul that would have killed her, if she were able to feel anything deeply. Vanessa Crofton shared a wound with John Hamdon, and it was all his fault. All of it. She needed to believe that.

Bast flew back to Chicago the same day. With the time zone change, he arrived in Chicago fifteen minutes after he left Cleveland.

He'd found what he was looking for, but he didn't

know what to do with it. John Hamdon really was a wounded animal. He was a lot—a *lot*—tougher than Bast ever thought. Bast had underestimated his opponent. And that never happened. He needed to be a lot more careful after this.

The wolf retched up nothing. His jaws hung open, dripping like a rabid animal's. The smell filled his head. The pain was blinding. He had to make it stop.

He ran toward the smell. He stumbled, crushed by the waves of pain—the worst ever. He got up. The drive to kill blotted out everything else.

Roll Call. 18 June 2012. 0800 hours.

The commander announced, "We have another dead-by-dog."

Jolted, John quickly looked to see if Bast was surprised. Bast only frowned. John wasn't sure he'd ever seen that expression on Bast. Bast's usually smooth brow was ridged. His head was down. He glowered from under that brooding brow.

The commander picked up the remote for his slide projector. "Fatal dog mauling, residential neighborhood. The victim was in his own home, in bed. The side door was open. Something—likely the dog—went through the screen. It left fur. It wasn't as careful this time."

He brought up the first slide. It showed a glum, round-faced man with a dark beard shadow. The picture was bad enough to be a mug shot or a driver's license photo.

"The victim is a fifty-one-year old male, Hap Sowacy.

Briefly married, long divorced. He lived alone in the residence for seven years. Did not own a dog. No criminal record. No mob connections. He was a part-time clown at children's birthday parties. And—" The commander projected a city map onto the wall with two points marked with red X's, "he lived on the opposite side of town from Manolo."

"Then why do we think this incident is related to Manolo's death?" Bast asked.

John sat straight up. *Why* wouldn't *we, Bast?*

The commander answered. "Because the victim's throat was ripped out, and the coroner puts the cause of death as asphyxiation, which is *not* consistent with throat ripping, but it *is* consistent with the Manolo killing. We have a possible serial killer."

Bast said, "But it's not a serial killer. It's a dog. Or more likely, dogs, since they're miles apart."

John looked at the ceiling. *There he goes. Trying to look completely past all the evidence again.*

The commander's face remained his normal granite mask. "The similarity of the two deaths is suspicious. But you're right, they're not necessarily connected. It's the same kind of wound, but this one didn't happen in a swimming pool, so brace yourselves, the scene is ugly." He projected another slide onto the wall.

John grunted. He heard sounds of disgust from everyone else except Chuck. Even Bast looked away, his eyebrows drawn way down.

"We have paw prints this time." The commander quickly clicked to the next slide.

"Ho! Big one!" Antwan cried.

The photo was of the paw print—in what looked like dried blood—with a ruler next to it for scale.

"Do you *shoe* a dog that size?" Meyers asked.

He's wearing shoes, John thought with a quick glance

behind him. *Black loafers with tassels.*

"Maybe our guided missile is freelancing now," Thea said. "He was trained for the first one. Second one, he likes it. He's doing what he knows."

Marv Meyers leaned over to talk to Bast. "You got a swamp monster down in Louisiana, don't you? A werewolf?"

"Loup-garou," Bast said, no trace of expression in his voice.

"Find the dog and find the owner," the commander barked, scanning the assembled detectives for someone to assign the case to.

John's eyes found the ceiling, as he tried to will himself invisible. He knew he was going to get this one again. He didn't want to work with Bast. *Find the dog. Find the dog. I think the dog is sitting behind me. How nuts am I?*

Antwan nudged John. "Cleveland, you're quiet."

"I'm creeped out." He also had his arms folded tight across his chest like a barricade.

"Cleveland," the commander called. "You and Bast."

John held in a groan. He walked up to take the preliminary report. He glanced inside the folder as he sat back down. "I know this address," he said. "Or close to it."

"Everyone knows that street," Thea said, looking over his shoulder, then turned around to tell Bast, "Take nose plugs."

"What's wrong with the street?" Bast asked on the way to Sowacy's house. John was driving. They were in a bland departmental sedan painted invisible brown.

"The neighborhood stinks," John said. "I mean that literally. There's a butcher shop on that block. The guy makes sausages and there are lots of complaints of the smell ruining the neighborhood."

The victim's home was a few doors down from the butcher's shop. The house was a dingy little dull yellow one-story still wearing the Bureau of Patrol's perimeter of yellow tape around the brown yard. Crime Scene had already been here and done their preliminary investigation.

John parked in the street in front of the yellow tape that stretched across the driveway. He opened the car door. "Oh, and there's that smell."

"It's not sausages," Bast said. "I wonder what the butcher is doing with the excess parts of the pig."

"Everyone wonders that," John said, slamming his door. "Health Department never found any code violations in the butcher's place. They've been out here enough times. They turned his shop inside out."

There was red tape over the side door of Sowacy's house for an inner perimeter. Bast had the keys. He opened the front door. John reeled back. "Wow." He instantly regretted opening his mouth. The air was thick enough to chew.

Bast kept his mouth closed. He narrowed his eyes and wrinkled his nose as if trying to shut out the smell.

The smell was a physical thing. John could feel it wrap around his skin. A hot day, a closed house, the stink just cooked in here.

John looked in the bedroom. The bed was stripped. Forensics had the bedding. There was a dried pool of blood on the floor with the hound of the Baskervilles' monster tracks in it. There were also human footprints in it, with no tread pattern. The Crime Scene investigators had to step in the blood to get to the victim.

The clown costume and gear was still in the closet—big red shoes, big red hair, big squirting plastic flower, bags of balloons. Crime Scene didn't think any of it was relevant to the dog attack. Bast loosened his tie and covered his nose with the front of his shirt.

John's hair always stood on end, but now it was prickling. "That smell is not from the sausage maker down the block."

"It's *here*," Bast said.

"Just how long was this guy dead before someone found him?"

Bast checked his copy of the prelim. "Two days."

This was a strong smell of decomp for the dead body being removed and the blood dry.

Evidence markers stood at each of the bloody paw prints. Crime Scene had lost the trail outdoors. There were scratches in the hard ground where the dog had cleaned its paws right outside the door. There hadn't been rain for a week, so there were no impressions in the parched brown grass.

John found a door with peeling white paint. "Did anyone look in the basement?"

Bast turned the page on the report. "Responding officers 'searched the premises.'" He let the sheet drop back on the report. "Doesn't say specifically basement. They were looking for a dog."

"Think it's worth another look down there?"

Bast opened the basement door. Immediately he moved back as if struck. His contorted face told John it was from the stench. Bast recovered, and spoke, opening his mouth as little as possible. "Yes, it's worth a look down there."

Maybe the killer hound was dead down there, John thought. Unless it was standing right here in front of him.

But Bast looked genuinely upset and apprehensive.

The light switch didn't work and there were no windows in the cellar. Bast and John descended into the cramped, claustrophobic space with their flashlights on. There were no paw prints on the steps, and no clean spots to say someone had erased any tracks.

The killer dog hadn't been down here. Maybe this was as far as Crime Scene got. John wanted to turn around and go back upstairs.

It was hard to breathe for the stench. The basement had the low ceilings of seventy years ago, before there was a height requirement in the building code. John and Bast were both tall, so neither of them could stand up straight. There were no bulbs in the bare sockets. The concrete walls were flaking. A thin industrial carpet was grimy and stiff underfoot, no telling what color it was supposed to be.

Bast's voice sounded strange—the voice of controlled fear. "John. Get out of here."

John immediately drew his gun and got his back against one moldering wall. "What?"

"Just leave."

John jammed his weapon back in his holster. "No."

He saw where Bast was standing. The hair on the back of Bast's head visibly lifted like hackles, his flashlight trained on the triangular space under the steps. John walked around to see what was under there.

Bags of cement and a shovel.

Crime Scene hadn't noted it. They had been looking for the dog that killed the homeowner. They had not been digging for evidence for something the homeowner may have done. This guy was the victim, not a suspect of something.

John wanted to say that the first responders were probably in a hurry to get out of this stinking dump, but he didn't want to open his mouth. The stench was strong enough to taste. Crime Scene had just made sure the dog was not on site, checked the entryways, looked for paw prints, bagged up the clown's bedroom, and got the hell out. John felt like running. Something turned inside his gut.

His gaze turned down, as if drawn, to the stiff carpet. John put on a glove and leaned down to pull up one corner.

"I wish you'd let me do that," Bast said.

"You know what's under here?" John asked.

"I know what this *bougre* did for living. I think I know what's under there."

Sowacy was a part-time clown at children's parties.

John pulled up the corner of the carpet and immediately dropped it. "Christ!" He grazed his head on the low ceiling as he jumped backwards.

Bast stepped forward, picked up the edge of the carpet and pulled it away, walking backwards as he revealed what was underneath.

There were rectangular depressions in the concrete floor. Rectangular holes had been dug, and refilled again. The top covers over the holes had settled a bit. The floor looked like a graveyard.

But the rectangles were too small.

"Do not hurl on the crime scene," Bast said.

John was going to be sick. It was the size that did it. Even though the size was right for dogs, he knew those weren't dogs under there. John spun and blundered up the wooden stairs.

Outside, he swallowed down sick. He managed not to throw up. His throat stung. His mouth burned sour.

He didn't want to leave Bast down there alone. Bast could be covering up evidence.

Cover up what? Bast didn't do that!

John palm-heeled moisture from his eyes, and stiffened his shoulders before Bast came out. John had thought he could take anything.

Bast stepped out to the curb, composed and stoic as a pallbearer. "You okay?'

"Fine."

Bast made the call to the Bureau of Patrol, reciting emotionless signal numbers.

The patrol car assigned to protect the scene wasn't far away.

John and Bast were at the crime scene until after sundown on one of the longest days of the year. By the time they were driving back to headquarters it was fully dark. Bast drove, grim-faced at the wheel.

A tremor came over John. That scene got him where it hurt. He wasn't going to make it. He double-tapped the door pillar with his palm. "Pull over."

Without question Bast pulled off the road by a tall fence that surrounded a manufacturing facility. John was opening the door before Bast even got the car to a complete stop.

A sudden wave of emotion overwhelmed John and he needed to cry—*not in front of Bast*.

John walked, enraged, breathing hard. *Keep it together, John.* He swung his arms as if loosening up for a fight. Bast stayed inside the car. John turned his face up at the merciless stars. *God. God. God.* How were such things allowed to be?

Gravel and dry grasses crunched under his soles. He dried his face on the backs of his hands.

He walked back to the car and let himself in. Bast waited, patient as a statue, straight-armed, with his fists on the wheel. John didn't think he'd moved except to set his teeth on edge. Bast's soft lips were in a hard set. He glowered straight ahead, his gaze fixed a million miles down the road.

"I'm ready," John said, fishing for his seatbelt.

"I'm not," Bast said. He sat back, let his hands drop to

his thighs, and exhaled. His eyes—there was something hurt and desperate in them—turned to John.

John wasn't sure who moved first after Bast unclicked his seatbelt.

John turned in his seat as both Bast's hands slipped behind his head to cradle it and draw him in to an open-mouth kiss. John closed his fists on Bast's jacket, kissing him back, fiercely. He needed to feel a heartbeat, heat, breath, and a human touch. He spied a glimmer that might have been tears on Bast's thick lashes. John got his hands inside Bast's jacket and ran his hands across Bast's chest.

In one motion Bast was out from under the steering wheel, out of his seat, and turning, lifting one long leg over the console to come down astride John's lap.

John tried to pull him closer as they kissed. It was difficult in the confines of the car. Bast was bent over, his head against the roof. John fumbled down at his side for the seat lever. Found it. The seat back fell back. Bast's weight fell forward on him. John's arms encircled him under Bast's jacket. Bast had no place to put his knees. And that brought John back to his senses. He pulled his arms back from around Bast's hard body and pushed. "Get off me."

Limber and smooth as a wraith, Bast was back in the driver's seat in a couple of racing heartbeats. John put his seat back up.

Mortified, John met Bast's gaze. Bast's dark eyes were opaque and unreadable.

John quickly looked away.

Awkwardness was a fat presence in the cabin, not just John's. Bast wasn't saying a word. The expected snotty, callus, careless barb didn't come. Bast had misplaced his giant ego somewhere.

And John. John had misplaced any crumb of sense he ever had.

Bast reached for his seatbelt. John pulled his own down, neither looking at the other. At least John wasn't looking, and he caught no head turns out of the corner of his eye from Bast. John fastened his belt as if it took all the concentration of brain surgery.

That did not just happen.

They drove the rest of the way in silence.

Bast stared at the bedroom ceiling. What made him kiss John? Was he trying to obliterate what he'd just seen by holding onto the man's strength? It had worked for a few fiery moments.

Just when he thought there could be no more waking nightmares, the shadows showed him new horrors. It used to be he never knew what the evil had done. He just had to kill it.

He'd thought he'd seen the worst, the lowest. The bottom just kept getting deeper.

Bast curled up in the bed. He'd lost a piece of his soul, if he still had one. He writhed in the sheets for desire of a man, trying to hold empty air. He tried to find some trace of John's scent on his hands.

Not what you're here for. Bast wanted him. His skin was singing for John's touch. His sex burned. He bit the air.

How did this bed get to be so empty?

He should never have kissed John Hamdon.

Chapter Four

Roll Call. 19 June 2012 0800 hours.

John sat on the opposite side of the room from Bast, not looking at him, not talking.

He told himself this wasn't high school. So John was embarrassed. So what? *Get the fuck over it and do your job.*

To make things worse, John had run into Graham Morris from Crime Scene on the way in. Morris took it personally that John uncovered the scene in Sowacy's cellar, as if John had gone out of his way to find something Crime Scene missed. Morris accused John of making him look bad. John told Morris to go look in the mirror if he wanted to see who did that.

The commander told the detectives of Central Investigations what they already knew—what was in Sowacy's cellar.

Twelve children.

"The FBI has taken charge of the case of the murdered children. The Feds think they're going to find other basements in two other states where Sowacy lived before Illinois. The dog mauling part of the case does *not* cross state lines. To the Feds, Sowacy's death is just a dog bite. Cleveland. Bast. You still have a case. The death—and possible murder—of Sowacy himself."

"I wouldn't look too hard for that killer," Georgia confessed. "I feel like giving him doggie treats."

The commander used his "wrath of God" voice.

"Detectives. I don't care if this pedophile monster—alleged pedophile monster—deserved to die. I want this dog. See if any of the victims' parents have a Rottweiler or a pit bull or a German Shepherd."

"No," John said.

The commander stared as if he could not have possibly heard correctly. "Excuse me, Detective?"

John went hot. "I am not investigating the families!"

"Oh, that's right. You're the wrong person to assign this to. Pitt—"

Thea Pittman-Jones, more quietly reasonable, said, "Sir, I'm with John. I'm not doing it. It's blaming the victims."

"Wallice—" the commander started over.

"I have a conflict," Chucky cut him off.

"What conflict?" the commander rumbled.

Chucky burbled into laughter. "I hate clowns." He dissolved into sniggering.

The commander turned his eyes heavenward. John thought the commander should know by now to expect shit out of Chuck. The commander said, "Cleveland, you're off anything to do with this case. Pitt, work with Animal Control to track down the dog."

Georgia asked, "Commander? Can a dog commit a crime?"

The commander opened and shut his mouth.

"I mean, it's a dog."

"It's a dangerous animal in my city! What has got into you? All of you!"

"Dead children, sir," Thea said very quietly.

The commander deflated. "Yeah," he breathed. In a moment he regrouped and growled, "There's a killer dog that could maul a child next time. Someone has to work the dog case."

"I'll go after the dog," John said. "But I'm not questioning the families."

Bast said, "No. I've got this. Commander's right. John, you shouldn't be on this case at all."

At the end of roll call John got up and walked out first, fuming. Behind him he heard the commander advising Bast, "Don't let the media turn this vicious dog into a hero. It's a monster whose victims just happened to also be monsters."

John was waiting for Bast as he came down the hall. John kept his voice low and demanded, "What do you mean I shouldn't be on this case?"

"You've had a tragedy," Bast said, his face averted. "I'm sorry."

John's mouth was full of pins. "I'm done beating myself up over Lori. She's not hurting anymore."

"I'm not talking about Lori," Bast said softly toward the floor.

"Everyone's got tragedies," John said. "You were in Katrina."

"You had *the* tragedy."

John felt blood leave his face. The bastard knew. *Son of a bitch. Son of a bitch. Son of a bitch.* "How do you know?"

"I Googled you."

"You more than Googled to get *that!*"

"*C'est vrai.*" It's true.

"Stay out of my life!"

Bast lifted his head high. "Stay out of mine, *cher*. I have this case."

"Great. Fine." John strode away. He gave the section door a mighty push. *Yeah, Commander. Give the case to the perp. Put Bast on the case. Bast* is *the case. Bast is a vigilante cop. And he has big paws.*

John jogged down four floors to the loading dock in back to take some breaths. It was gray and shitty out here, trying to rain.

Check yourself, John. You thought you saw this guy and a wolf under your car. That's the whole basis for your conviction. Back it off, son.

Still, Bast felt wrong. *I know he's wrong. And he scares the shit out of me.*

John hadn't been afraid of anything since the worst happened.

A motion made him look over to the side. He was surprised to see Thea on the other side of the loading dock. She stood with her arms tightly crossed. John called over to her. "What are you doing out here?"

"Pretending I'm a smoker," Thea said. Her normally smooth mellow voice sounded scratchy. She'd been crying. "You?"

"Smoking out my ears."

Thea nodded. She wiped away a tear. "Anyone even *thinks* about touching Bron and Kayla, I'll pull his arms off."

John sucked in a breath between gritted teeth. "Not their arms, I think."

"Yes, well, I don't like to talk like that," Thea said primly, but John could hear it unspoken—anyone threatened Thea's kids, the nuts would for sure be coming off that tree.

And John thought of Daniel. His little boy was never far from his thoughts.

John had been teaching him how to hit the tee ball when John's marriage to Daniel's mother fell apart.

John was playing for the Akron Aeros in the minors when he married Vanessa Wilson. Vanessa had visions of being the wife of a Major League ball player. And John had married her because she looked like the wife of a Major League ball player. She wanted him to take the steroids if it would get him into the bigs. Instead, John followed his father into the Cleveland Police Department.

John wasn't sure who cheated first. Vanessa lost interest in sex—with him anyway. John was pretty sure she was getting satisfied elsewhere. But he was the one who got caught. The lipstick was not on his collar.

He'd done it with a hooker. You can never disappoint a hooker. They get what they want out of you in advance.

With spectacular speed the locks on the house were changed, the bank account emptied, and Vanessa had a lawyer. Half the money came back in time, but as soon as the separation was signed, Lloyd Crofton moved into the house.

Then at the custody hearing, Vanessa had the balls to use Lloyd Crofton to claim she could give Daniel a complete home—a mother and a father and the house Daniel knew.

So John got to pay child support to a guy who shacked up with his wife in his own house. Lloyd and Vanessa used the child support money to hire babysitters instead of calling John to watch Daniel when they were at work or when they ate out, which was often. John knew this because Daniel called him when they were out and asked him to come over. John had done that. Once.

After that Daniel's voice on the phone tore his heart out. "Why can't you come overrr?"

"Just can't." John couldn't possibly explain the concept of "restraining order" to his son. Vanessa told the court she was afraid John would kidnap Daniel. And that was starting to sound like a brilliant idea.

Lloyd didn't even try to adopt Daniel. Vanessa and Lloyd hadn't asked John to give up Daniel. The answer would have been "hell, no" of course, but it pissed John off to know that Daniel was living with a guy who didn't want him.

So John got online to find countries that didn't have extradition rights with the U.S. Kidnapping Daniel and moving to Venezuela was looking better and better. *We could star on a milk carton together.* As soon as he figured out how to make a living in Venezuela, he was going to make that happen. In the meantime, John never failed to show up for his Wednesday and every other weekend.

Never.

Roll Call. 2 July 2012. 0800 hours.

Everyone was in attendance. It was an inspection day. There were no uniforms in this unit. Still the detectives had to dress according to the regs. The commander told Bast his hair was too long again.

Then the commander called for case updates. "Bast. Dogs."

There was no woofing this time. It wasn't remotely funny anymore.

"*Je suis foutu.*"

"In English, Detective Bast?"

"I'm fucked. We got dog hair and tracks this time, but nothing to match them to. I got nothing to connect the two cases and nothing to definitely rule a connection out. I got nothing."

"Write it up," the commander said resignedly. "Park it. Wait for a third one not to happen."

Bast gave a single nod. "Yes, sir."

John muttered aside to Bast. "Did you get all your tracks covered?"

"Not sure." Bast leaned in close to John. "Tell me, does my breath smell like clown?"

John put his hand on Bast's face and pushed him away.

Bast's breath actually smelled enticing.

After roll call, during the murmur and shuffle of

detectives rising from their seats, Bast told John in a confidential voice. "To tell the truth, I did find an exact match to the dog hair."

The meaning of what Bast just said took its own sweet time sinking into John's skull. He couldn't believe what he just heard. He dogged Bast out of the conference room and down the hall. He whispered, "You falsified your report?" That was a strange thing to confess to a guy who was trying to take him down. "Why are you telling me that?"

"The match is already in the evidence locker," Bast said carelessly. "From the Internal Affairs investigation of your accident." His dark brows lifted and his full lips formed a secretive smile. "It's the dog hair from under your car."

That rocked John off center. He felt light headed. Quills of fear prickled under his tongue. It was a set up. Bast had put the dog hair under his car. *I'm being set up.*

And I kissed you, you mo fo.

He needed to take down Bast now.

John had to burn two vacation days to get to New Orleans.

He took a bus down Thursday and a bus back Saturday. On the Friday in between, he visited the precinct where Bast had supposedly worked. He found out Bast really did work for the New Orleans Police Department between 2007 and 2011. The people John interviewed loved Bast. That made asking suspicious questions tough. John asked after records from where Bast was before 2007.

"Oh. René come from Terrebonne Parish." The admin laughed. She had an open face. Her nail polish was chipped. The hem of one sleeve of her blouse was held up with a staple. She had a pretty voice. Her name was Susz. "You want those records? Go fish. That be the Bayou. You won't find records there."

Katrina, again.

John asked Susz if she had any cases two years ago or older of people who had their throats torn out by a giant dog.

Her brow creased and her mouth pulled to one side in thought. "No. Nothing like that. But we did have a rash of really strange bite cases. These people were bitten on the ear. There musta been two dozen or more. Most of them said they were bit by a wolf, but one of them—I saw it—that was human bite. But it was on the ear, not the throat. He said he was bit by a werewolf. And it stole his car."

"Did Bast work the case?"

"I don't think René was with us yet. No. No, he wasn't."

"Did anyone swab the bites for DNA evidence?"

"You really aren't from around here. We really didn't have the resources."

Katrina. He had to sound like a real asshat.

An officer walked over to Susz's desk. He must have overheard their conversation. "You talking about our vampire?"

"Vampire?" John said. "Does he—the biter—does he have pronounced canines? You know?" John hooked two fingers in front of his mouth to indicate fangs.

"No. This nut has ordinary teeth. Pretty good ones at that."

Bast does have a dazzling smile.

Susz nodded agreement with that. "It was a really neat bite. Nice arch. We're not looking for a meth case."

The officer gave a dismissive snort. He obviously considered the case dead cold. "We're not looking at all."

I'm afraid we are. He crossed state lines. He's our nut now.

Returning to work Monday morning, John got waylaid in the parking lot by Bast. Bast's hair was looking too long again. It was starting to curl. He wore a white shirt, dove gray jacket, and dusky trousers. He said lazily, "You have a hard-on for me, John. *Porquois?*"

Did he know John had been in New Orleans? John bypassed the question and went on the offense. "What are you?"

"A Cubs fan?" Bast suggested innocently.

"You should not have lived."

"You say the sweetest things. But I don't understand, *cher.*"

John lowered his voice. "I *did* run you over with my car." Crazed memory or not, he knew what he'd seen. He'd hit the wolf. He'd seen Bast under his car.

"Did you?" Bast said gently—the voice you use with Great Aunt Martha when she calls you to look at the elephants in the backyard.

"I know what I saw. And so do you."

Bast laughed softly, a maddeningly sexual sound. "Do you try to tell anyone that?"

"No."

Bast nodded. "I wouldn't advise it. I'm glad you're here. I need to ask you about Lori."

John's insides seized up. "Leave it," he said, vibrating fit to detonate. "Just. Don't."

Bast asked anyway. "Had she been smoking?"

Not a question John was expecting. In fact it was a really bizarre question. "No—" he started. His voice came to an abrupt stop on a sudden thought. He questioned just how bizarre Bast's question was.

"But?" Bast prompted. "I heard a 'but' in there. She wasn't smoking, but what?"

"Nothing," John said walking toward the entrance. He mumbled to himself, "Seeing things."

"I thought so."

John spun round, angry. "What?"

"Nothing," Bast said. "Just the blackness."

"All right!" John stalked toward Bast. "Stop jerking me around. What do you know about Lori?"

John had been told he was formidable when he was pissed, but Bast was unfazed. "Do not fuck with me, *cher*," Bast said, matter-of-fact. "Just tell me what I need to know."

"You need! You are a real piece of work, you know that?"

"I am so aware of that. Talk to me. About the darkness you weren't going to tell anyone about."

"Tell what? I thought I saw something black. That's it. I got hit in the face with an airbag and cracked my head on the asphalt and then I saw a black cloud that wasn't there. Nothing to report."

"Exactly where did you see it come from? What did it do? Where did it go?"

"Do? What does smoke do? I was not really focused on the fucking smoke—*if* I really saw it. I had other things on my mind. LIKE MY DEAD GIRLFRIEND. What aren't *you* telling *me*?"

John's own heaving breaths sounded loud to him. He waited for an answer, staring. He had to look crazed.

Bast looked down the half-inch he had on John. He might as well be gazing down from a mountaintop, his face otherworldly, calm, and lineless. "Everything," Bast said.

John followed the GPS directions to Bast's address. He knew from a web crawl on the Cook County Assessor's site that Bast had got the property cheap on a short sale. John wanted to see if it was really where Bast lived or just the address he used for his residency requirement.

When he arrived, he double checked the address. He'd been expecting a derelict, boarded-up shell. He was surprised to find a neat little house with a fresh coat of Cajun red paint, a new roof, a trim lawn on what little real estate there was in the tiny yard. There were new, black, New Orleans style wrought-iron filigree bars over the door and windows. It wasn't just an address. It really was a residence. And Bast wasn't living large, not here anyway.

The house was built on a slab. It had no basement. That was very New Orleans, but it was alien to John. *Where do you put your junk?* It had a one-car detached garage with no windows, so John couldn't tell if Bast's car was in there or not.

John hadn't expected a real residence. Now that he was here, he didn't want to run into Bast. But he wasn't going to be seen just driving away either. That would make him look like a stalker, when actually, he was a stalker.

Okay. Be casual. I'm supposed to be here. He parked blatantly in the driveway, walked up to the front door, and rang the bell. And if Bast was here? *Well, then bunt.* He waited. His heartbeat slowed down as no footsteps sounded in answer to the bell.

He glanced around, then jimmied the lock on the iron door and the new front door and let himself in.

It should've struck him wrong that Bast didn't have the deadbolt engaged. John shut the door behind him.

And oh shit fuck damn screw, Bast has a dog.

Big one.

Big *big* one that looked like a wolf. Its mouth was open in a kind of smile, and oh grandma, those were big teeth. It had coarse, pepper-black fur and a slow-wagging, bushy tail.

John swallowed. His still-intact throat felt tight.

He wanted to reach for his gun. It was secured in the car.

He slowly backed out the door. The wolf advanced with his retreat, its brown eyes looking up at him. John drew the door shut and made sure the catch clicked. He shut the iron gate over the front door and forced himself to move no faster than a walk to his car.

Before roll call, John sauntered to where Bast sat reading the latest directive and drinking coffee in the break room. "Detective Bast."

"Detective Hamdon," Bast said, without looking up from his handheld.

"You didn't tell me you had a dog."

"I don't."

John re-phrased, "You didn't tell me you had a wolf."

"I don't."

John was not going to play word games. "Whatever you want to call it, I know your beast is behind those killings. Manolo. Sowacy."

"I assure you I own no beast."

"I feel so assured."

"You saw a big dog?"

"Yeah. I did. In your house."

"Did you take it outside and run it over?"

"You suck."

"Been known to. But only if I really like you."

As John was stalking out, he heard Bast's voice at his back. "John?"

John turned and snapped, impatient. "What?

"Do you ever wonder if you're gay?"

That was the last thing John expected to come out of Bast's mouth. Still, he knew that kiss was going to come back around and bite him sometime.

"No," John said.

"Me neither. I never wonder."

"Good to know. I was so worried," John said. "What kind of moosedick question is that anyway?" *Do you ever wonder if you're gay?* "Now if I thought I was a Cubs fan I'd have a problem."

John avoided Bast for the rest of the day. He mentioned Bast's pet to no one. John knew that, even if he could get someone to believe him, the wolf wouldn't be in Bast's house when Patrol showed up at the door with a warrant.

At the end of the day, the section headed to the parking lot in a pack.

A street woman with a wild nest of hair had wandered off the sidewalk and in between the bollards that surrounded HQ. She stared at the detectives like a psych case. She lifted a bony, quaking finger at them and said, "Evil is here. It's in here. It is...."

Her finger was shaking so badly she could have been pointing at any of them or the man in the moon.

"Here," John finished for her, pointing at Bast. "Got your evil right here."

Bast checked inside his breast pocket for hidden evil and said, "I don't think so." He turned to Meyers. "Do you have it?"

John inhaled to say something else but he took in a gnat. He coughed several times, brought his fist to his chest, swallowed, and said in a strangled voice, "Ah hell, could be in here."

Georgia stepped forward and took the street woman's hands. "Ma'am, do you need help finding a shelter for the night?" But the woman pulled back her hands and tottered away, muttering.

The detectives fanned out to their separate cars. John kept walking through the lot to the street. He heard fast-clumping footsteps catching up with him. He turned and instantly wished it was a mugger. It was Chuck Wallice. John turned and kept on walking.

John could only *just* stand to be in the same room as Chuck.

Chuck fell in step with him. "You going out for faster action, Cleveland?"

"No, I'm going to catch a bus," John said. He crossed the street, trying to lose Chuck. But Chuck kept up with him. Chuck was talking. John wasn't listening until Chuck suddenly veered off, saying, "Oh, look at that."

John had to look. Chuck was marching back across the street to where a woman in a bright red crop top, a tiny leather skirt, and four-inch heels was bending over a car's driver side window. John could see home plate from here.

Chuck was not a beat cop, but he pulled out his star. The driver took off at Chuck's approach, and the woman turned.

Oh hell, Chuck was going to arrest her. *Oh, but that's not a legal search and seizure there, Chucker*. One part of John knew he should just stay out of it, but the other part of John Hamdon was crossing the street.

Chuck had apparently offered to give the hooker a pass, because he took her by the elbow and said, "Come here and we'll talk about it." He was headed toward a dark service entrance behind a building.

John groaned. Chuck was going to take it out in trade.

I hate this shit.

The woman looked of age, and she wasn't looking to John for help. She had a let's-get-this-over-with sneer on her face.

Chuck glanced over one brawny shoulder at John. "You got my back, right?"

John waved a hand down behind him and walked away. *To hell with you.* John wanted nothing to do with him. He didn't even know what the hell Chuck was going to do with a hooker. Nuts that size don't work.

Then he heard the woman's screech.

What the hell!

John came running back.

He found them behind the dumpster. He stalked forward, seized Chuck's burly shoulders and pulled him off. "That's enough."

Chuck turned, his eyes round with shock and rage. He was fully clothed. "You—!"

John barked to the woman, who was staggering onto her spike heels. "Get out of here." Before she could flip her short skirt down, he saw blood high inside her thigh.

"Fuckers!" she spat. John turned away just in time for her pepper spray to spatter the back of his head. The woman stumbled away.

Chuck was bug-eyed in a speechless rage. There was a touch of blood on his cheek. When Chuck could talk he whispered with a forced smile, wagging a finger at John. "Oh. Paybacks. Paybacks."

Chapter Five

John had never been to this diner before. He was meeting his section for breakfast on Sunday morning. The gathering was Marv Meyers' idea. Meyers hadn't so much invited John as urgently requested his presence.

John had changed out of his sweats from his morning workout. He wore a plain gray tee-shirt and blue jeans. He didn't want to be in sweats if Bast was going to be there. He couldn't trust his cock to stay down.

As he walked in, he saw that almost everyone else was already there. Bast looked ever-so fine in light khaki cargo pants and a black, short-sleeved polo. It was the first time John got to see Bast's arms. They were sleekly muscled. The hair on his forearms was dark. Bast wore a gold necklace and a gold stud in his right ear. John hadn't noticed him having a piercing before.

Georgia coached girls' soccer on Sundays. She was dressed in her red and yellow striped jersey, and wore a whistle on a lanyard around her neck, ready to go to practice after this breakfast.

Thea had her two-year-old daughter, Kayla, on her knee. Thea looked surprised as John walked up to the table. "You look like hell."

"Thanks," John dragged a chair to the table. "You don't."

"You okay?" Antwan asked, making room for him.

John nodded into his hand. "Tired." Some days he couldn't get out of his own way. He'd only done half a workout this morning, and just that was a struggle.

Georgia asked, "You sleeping okay?"

"Like a rock." He'd slept straight through the night last night. He didn't dream.

This was Meyers' show. After the coffee was poured and their orders put in, he signaled them all to draw in so he didn't need to speak loud. He leaned over the table. "Organized Crime is saying they're progressing better against Krieg's network without us."

He left a silence for them to absorb the full significance of that. Antwan translated, "They're saying one of us is feeding tip-offs to Krieg."

"No, that's what they're *not* saying," Meyers said meaningfully.

"They're *not* saying it real, real loud," John said.

"Yeah," Meyers said.

The Organized Crime Division had brought the Central Investigations Section in to work with them on the Krieg case. Together OCD and CIS had deployed a string of foolproof maneuvers to catch Krieg in the act of receiving drug shipments. The maneuvers had gone completely south. The drug shipments didn't exist.

The Organized Crime Division had just informed the Criminal Investigations Section that their assistance was no longer required on the Krieg case.

One person was absent from this party.

John looked around. "Where's the Chucker?"

Bast sneezed. "*Tchu.*"

"You want him?" Thea said.

"No." John had thought this was a section meeting.

Then he realized, yes, it was a section meeting. It was just that Chuck was not invited. That's why they were at a new diner.

Meyers was asking Bast, "Are you allergic to Chuck? You always sneeze when someone says his name."

"I'm not sneezing, *cher*. I'm calling him an asshole."

"In that case, bless you," Meyers said.

"Hey!" Georgia said, an objection.

Bast said, "Anyone like the Chuck for our leak?"

"I like you for it," John said back.

"I know you do, John."

"That's right. I forgot," John said. "You're a mind reader."

"*Cher*, cloistered monks in Tibetan monasteries know you think it's me."

"I don't think it's any of us," Georgia said. "OCD is wrong."

John shook his head, his smile crooked over to one side. "Gotta love ya, George. Count on you to say 'yay, team' when we're down eleven to zip in the ninth inning."

"I love you too, John," Georgia said. She meant it.

"Group hug," Meyers said.

"Bite me," John said, then quickly to Bast. "Not you. You'll do it."

Antwan crossed his boulder-muscled forearms on the table and leaned forward. His eyes shifted left and right. "What if George is right? It's not any of us? There's a lot of civilians in the office."

"They haven't been read into the operation," Meyers said. "I admit Chucky's not the covert type. He's as subtle as a toilet seat. Chucky gets his rocks off on violence."

"Chucky don't got rocks to get off," John said. He caught all of them staring at him. "What? Am I the only guy who cops a glance in the men's room to see what the other team's got?"

"*Yeah*," Antwan declared with a defensive side shift, shielding his own jewels.

Meyers returned to business. You knew the serious was deep if Meyers was serious. "I don't like the guy—"

"He's a *crotte*," Bast said.

"Probably," Meyers said. "I don't know what that

means but it sounds nasty enough. Let's say he's a *crotte*. But I gotta tell ya, I don't see Chucky selling out."

Antwan drew his lips in tight so he was almost wincing, and he had to nod to that. "He's like ninety-second generation cop."

"Well, who else is there?" Thea threw it out there.

"The commander," Antwan said.

"I'd suspect *me* before I suspected the commander," John said.

Antwan nodded. "But that's all of us."

Meyers said, "That's the thing. I know it's not one of us. I don't *think* it's Chuck, but someone is tipping Krieg off."

"Unless..." John started speculative, following a half-formed thought. "Unless Chuck is only leaking information to Krieg to set us up to fail so he can break the case all by himself and be the hero."

Thea's gracefully shaped brows arched high. "That's pretty fanciful, John."

But even Georgia had to admit, "It does kinda sound like him."

"I like it," Meyers said. "That could be the angle I'm missing."

Thea bounced little Kayla on her knee. "I would love to like Chucky for this. I mean I really truly *truly* would. But I just don't."

John elbowed Bast. "Read his mind, Bast. See if it's Chuck."

"I don't want to touch him," Bast said. "He's a pig."

"Don't slander the pigs," Thea said.

"Tweee!" Georgia said, and she tossed a yellow card onto the table to signal foul.

Thea was never one for insults, so John smelled an unreported harassment incident in that one. Thea didn't defend herself. She slapped Georgia's yellow card right back down on the table in front of Georgia, and looked on the verge of showing Georgia which finger she wore her Olympic ring on.

They paused their discussion as their breakfast orders arrived. Then Bast said, "I don't like guessing. I'm going to talk to him."

"*You*'re going to talk to Chuck?" Meyers asked, surprised.

"To Krieg."

John's coffee found its way into his saucer. Antwan dropped his bagel.

Thea ducked her head at Bast and looked at him out of the tops of her eyes. "Really?"

"Sure," Meyers said, looking like Bast had just invited him to dance the Lobster Quadrille. "Just walk in and chat with the crime boss."

John put up his hand, volunteering. "I'll go with."

Bast translated the gesture. "You don't trust me."

"I do," John vowed, hand over heart. *Almost to the very tips of my eyelashes.* He was not going to let the department's leak update his boss without a witness. Out loud he said, "We don't have orders."

Bast took his ID and star from one of his pockets and tossed them on the table. "I'm just a citizen paying a call to another citizen."

John drew his own and tossed them down on top of Bast's. "Road trip."

Thea gathered in their IDs and stars. "I'll hang onto these."

"OCD is going to have kittens," Georgia said.

Meyers' face took on a look of major league concern, and John sensed that he and Bast were about to get a stern wave off. But Meyers turned the back of his head toward them, pretending nothing was happening. He leaned his cheek on his fist and said to Georgia, "And how's Lacey doing on the soccer team this year?"

John felt a strange twinge getting into the car with Bast. It was Bast's own car, not a city vehicle. It was like entering Bast's lair.

Bast's car was a weirdly shaped dinosaur of a twenty-year-old maroon Saab. The gauges were round and made the dashboard look like the cockpit of an old aircraft. It was manual transmission with a gear shift between the seats. There wouldn't be any climbing over the console on this ride, though Bast was pretty damn limber.

The twangy music wasn't from the radio. It was a muddy recording of a lively accordion and fiddle and something that sounded suspiciously like a washboard and a triangle. "What the hell kind of mush singing is that?" John said. "This guy mumbles worse than you. I can't understand a word."

"I'd be surprised if you could, *cher*. It's Cajun."

John growled, but caught his foot tapping on the floor board.

Bast was ball-achingly beautiful in casual clothes, with the wind in his hair, his shirt open at his throat. Sunglasses could make almost any man look sexy. They made Bast look absolutely lethal.

"Bast?"

"Yes, John."

"Does Krieg know you?"

"I don't know."

John couldn't see Krieg's house from the road as Bast drove up to the gate, but he could just glimpse the turrets over the treetops.

Bast stopped at the gatehouse and told the guard.

"René Bast and John Hamdon to see Krieg."

"Is Krieg expecting you?"

"Hard to say," Bast said.

Waiting, John kept his head still, but his eyes moved behind his sunglasses, searching for snipers. *We're gonna get murdered.*

It surprised him when the tall iron gates parted and the guard waved them in.

Bast put the car in gear and started forward up a very long driveway. The colored pavers made it look like the Saab was rolling up the back of a giant, diamondback rattlesnake.

The heavily treed grounds cleared to the mansion that had to be visible from outer space.

Two hulking man-things who looked like professional wrestlers stepped down the snowy white marble steps from the palatial front door. John could scarcely see the holster bulges under their expertly tailored suit jackets. This was private property. They could carry whatever they wanted.

Bast and John got out of the car.

At a head nod from Thing One, Bast took a wide stance and spread his arms for a pat down.

John stared at Thing Two, who had no neck and probably couldn't make a head motion, so he just stared at John, waiting for him to assume the position.

John balked. "I'm not getting searched."

"You want to wait in the car?" Bast asked.

You wish. John spread his arms. The crotch search wasn't as bad as he expected. Thing Two didn't want his hand there either.

The guards escorted Bast and John to the monumental redwood door, and handed them off to an immaculately groomed, steel-haired, suntanned majordomo who smelled costly.

John expected to be parked in a broom closet to wait. And wait. Normally the more important the person thought he was, the longer the wait to see him. He and Bast could be here for days.

They were taken straight into the presence.

That meant Krieg really wanted to see one of them.

Gee. Wonder which one.

John meant to pay close attention to Krieg's face as he first set eyes on Bast, but what John saw when they passed through the doors was so frikkin' weird he forgot all about where he meant to look.

Not sure what struck him first: the giant swastika taking up most of one soaring wall or that Krieg was blue.

He was not the blue of the good guys in *Avatar*. Krieg's skin was that sick shade of gray-blue that came from eating silver. It was some kind of a health fad that wasn't healthy at all.

Krieg was a balding man with a vast belly, dressed in shorts and sandals, and throned in a thickly padded, white leather chair, oversized to accommodate him. He was shirtless, leaving his chest with its shag of gray-white hair and floppy man-boobs on show. He wore so many silver chains John couldn't see his neck. The weird color to his skin and his lips was mesmerizing.

Krieg's gaze shifted from Bast to John and back to Bast and back to John.

John couldn't read his expression. If anything, Krieg looked puzzled.

The look on Bast's face was startling. Bast looked like he was having a migraine.

Krieg's eerie gaze finally settled on Bast. Frowning and wary, Krieg said, "Un-ex-pec-ted."

John had no idea what Krieg meant. John got the idea that Krieg's comment wasn't for them anyway. The giant slug was just talking to himself.

Bast seemed to be in pain, but John could tell that Bast had been expecting what he saw—kind of.

Krieg's weird-colored eyelids closed and opened. John thought his body paint would crease but it wasn't paint. That really was his skin color. Krieg spoke again, "Is this about that parking ticket?" He pitched a large coin at Bast.

Bast pivoted back like a door opening to let the coin fly past him.

When the coin stopped spinning and dropped flat on the snowy marble floor John looked back to see it was a Morgan silver dollar.

Bast didn't bother telling Krieg that he and John weren't traffic cops. Krieg probably knew that.

"I am here for your wisdom," Bast said as if consulting a silver Buddha, his voice steady despite his migraine. "You know a lot. You're almost clairvoyant. You know things before they happen."

"And?" Krieg said, cautiously. He looked off balance, confused.

Bast said, "And I want to punch out your all-seeing eye."

Okay, John could almost see where Bast was going here. Bast was angling for Krieg to confirm that he actually had someone working for him within the Chicago Police Department.

Krieg took his time forming an answer. Again he looked from Bast to John and back to Bast. "Wouldn't that be assault and battery?"

The way Krieg tiptoed around Bast's questions, John got a sudden mental image of those dancing hippos in tutus in the Disney flick. John didn't know this dance. But it was clear that these two had history.

Bast said, "It would be much worse than that."

John suddenly wondered if Bast was threatening—or offering—to kill the police snitch. It sure sounded like that was what he was saying.

Krieg leaned back. He put up his hands in a kind of surrender and let them fall as if conceding. "Do it then."

Bast suddenly dropped the hinting and feinting. He came right out and demanded, pained and angry, "Who you got?"

There was a startled instant of silence, then Krieg boomed laughter, big and lusty and genuine. Krieg's apprehension vanished. He acted like he'd just been dealt a fourth ace.

His laughter got bigger and louder. And yes, he really did slap his pudgy knee.

The gales subsided. Krieg kept grinning, beaming at Bast. That was a man sitting on a very funny secret. Krieg wiped away some tears, then gave a back-handed wave with his doughy hand. "Get out of here."

The impeccable majordomo stepped forward but Bast was already heading for the door. John followed.

When they passed through the huge entryway into sunlight, John was relieved to see Bast's car was still there. Thing One and Thing Two were standing on either side of it like Secret Service agents.

Bast got down on the pavement, Spiderman style, to look under his car. He checked in the trunk, under the hood, and under the steering column before he got in. He pushed the passenger side door open for John.

Driving away over the paved snake's back, Bast glowered over the wheel. John was really on guard now. That weird interchange all but proved Bast was in tight with Krieg's network. And it looked like Krieg had just cut Bast out of the ring.

Once the car was through the gate and on the road beyond sight of any security camera, John said, an accusation, "You know each other."

"We met a couple times," Bast said, tight. A long silence stretched between them. John waited for him to add some details to that. At last Bast said, "It buried me alive."

"It? You mean him?"

Bast's voice vibrated low. "John, that is an *it*."

John guessed Krieg must've screwed Bast over pretty good during his New Orleans days. John wasn't aware that Krieg had tentacles in New Orleans.

"Yeah. I agree. That was an it," John said. "I don't like the way he—it—was looking at me."

"I don't either," Bast said. "Krieg wants me to think he has someone in the department."

John said, "But that's already what we think isn't it?"

Bast pressed his lips tight together, eyebrows high, and nodded. "Who? I missed a turn somewhere."

"I'm still good for it being you." Again, he waited. Finally John asked, "Aren't you going to deny it?"

"It's not me," Bast said, then glanced aside at John. "Do you believe me?"

"No."

Bast gave a shrug as someone who has just jumped through a useless hoop.

"How's your head?" John asked. Bast's migraine seemed to have vanished.

"I'm all right."

Bast was not what John would call "all right." He had no right being that seductive. He was easy and hard to be with. John fought a strong attraction, even as a sense of mortal danger crawled up his spine.

John asked, "Did you come to Chicago because Krieg is here?"

"Yes."

Wow. A straight answer. "Can we stop the twenty

questions and you just tell me what you're about?"

"No."

"Okay. Just how come a crime lord of Krieg's power gives a rat's ass what you think, Detective Bast?"

"I don't think he does," Bast said, distracted. "I messed up somewhere."

"You're way off the grid," John said. "At best, you're a vigilante. I'm going to turn you in."

Bast scarcely reacted. "That would be sad, *cher*. You got nothing."

Bast had to be the leak to Krieg. But it looked like Bast and Krieg were seriously on the splits now. Bast wouldn't be leaking any more information. John was not going to be able to make his accusation stick. Bast was right, John had nothing.

Later in the week, John and Bast were alone in the section offices on the fourth floor after hours, cleaning up case reports. They were both behind on paperwork.

Bast had come up with a dead end finding the dog that killed the pedophile, Sowacy. And John had failed to come up with anything that Bast missed or covered up—except that Bast had a big black wolf he wasn't mentioning. That was a big hairy thing.

Angry, frustrated, John let himself into Bast's office and gazed out the window, silently fuming. The smug son of a bitch was just sitting there, draped back in his chair, feet on the desk under his vast mirror. John resented his good looks and his magnetism. Bast made John burn. In so many ways.

Rain tapped at the windowpane and trickled down like tears.

Bast was talking, so softly John was not aware of his

starting. It was not him breaking the silence so much as he wafted out of it in his soft Cajun accent, speaking impossibilities.

"The shadow was lodged. The man was gone. We try to catch them before they become embedded. Once the humanity is gone there's no point being neat about it. You need to make sure you get the shadow. Keep it in there until the body is dead. They try to escape through the throat."

It was all pure insanity. John didn't even understand what Bast was saying, except John heard bare truth in it.

Shadow. That made him think of the dark shapes he'd see on the road and around Lori.

They. That was horrifyingly plural.

We. Who was *we*?

Questions were piling up behind John's eyes like a wreck on the Dan Ryan in an ice storm.

Bast had gone quiet again. He was sitting way back, three long fingers propping up an elegant cheekbone, the other hand hanging indolently over the arm of the chair. A catlike presence, he seemed at the same time young and ancient, vibrant and listless. Deadly. Unreal.

Real as a kick in the nads.

John couldn't believe Bast was telling him this.

The tapping rain pushed to the foreground in the thick quiet.

"I was chasing one the night we met," Bast said at last. "We met hard."

"I hit a dog," John said from somewhere in the twilight zone.

"No, you didn't. You hit me."

A strange relief came over John. Bast finally admitted it. *I'm not nuts. I wasn't seeing things.* Everything John knew was true was validated at last.

By a lunatic.

"What do you do with a—" John had a hard time making himself saying it, it was so insane, "—shadow when you catch up with it?"

"If it's lodged, I trap it in the host and kill it. If it's loose, inhale it. Consume it. Destroy it."

"You've been inhaling something, that's for damn sure."

"It's simple, really. It's the eternal war at twilight. Light and dark cannot stand together. One ceases to exist. I intend to exist."

"Which are you?"

"Which do you think?"

"I'm gonna go home and sleep off whatever acid I dropped that makes me think we're having this conversation."

John was not going to tell anyone about this conversation. *I'll sound crazed.* Bast had to be setting him up to sound crazed. Trouble was John didn't believe that anymore. There was raw honesty in that quiet, impossible confession.

Now I know. And he couldn't do a damn thing with it. Bast had the easiest secret in the world to keep. *It's totally crackers.*

When John got home, the doubts returned. His apartment was wonderfully mundane, ordinary, and real. Belief in men who could turn into wolves and chase evil shadows could not persist amid vinyl tiles, laminate countertops, and microwave ovens.

I saw that man under my car. How do you explain that, John?

He didn't have to explain it. There was trick in there somewhere. John didn't see what he thought he saw. *I didn't see him under the car. He's playing to my delusion.*

Bast was pulling him by the short hairs. *What I really have is a vigilante cop who I—and only I—know is dirty.*

Chasing Shadows

And he's got a pet wolf trained to kill.

How on Earth could he report that? Bast was easy going. The section loved him. He was clinically insane and everyone thought he was a great guy. He was probably the ear biter of New Orleans. No one would believe John if he reported what Bast said back there. *And I half believe him! What does that make me?*

Well, there was one question with an easy answer. *Foutu.*

After work the next day, John was heading out to his car when Bast beckoned him toward a stairwell in the parking garage. "Come here. I want to show you something."

"Is this what it sounds like?" John asked.

"More or less." Bast slipped behind the metal door.

John hung back a moment. He didn't want his throat ripped out. On the other hand, he was sure he could take Bast down. That decided it. *Hell, I'm game.*

John followed him through the doorway.

Bast stood under the stark lights. "John. Can I flash you?"

"Flashers don't ask."

"I'm asking."

"Hey. Bring it." John stepped back, ready to be awed by Bast's prodigious manhood.

In one blink the clothes were falling. All of them. A pepper-black wolf stood beside them.

John stumbled over his own feet, reeling backwards. *"Shit!"* Turning, he caught himself against the white-painted cinderblock wall. He looked back over his shoulder.

There was Bast, in a crouch, naked, collecting his

clothes. He had a strong, narrow build. From out of the thick, dark hair in his groin, a long, white erection stood up. It was pretty. Bast looked up through thick lashes. "You don't look so good, *cher*."

"I've lost my grip on reality."

Bast straightened up to step into a red thong. "Would you like a drink?"

"No. I want my grip back."

"No," John said out loud. He hadn't meant to. He was alone. He just wanted the thought out of his head.

It was still there.

I'm hot for a vigilante werewolf.

He paced his one-bedroom apartment from end to end.

You don't even like him.

He stalked to the entrance door.

Yeah, you do.

He paced to the fire escape—

He's fucking with you.

And into the kitchen.

He's not human. That's a deal breaker right there.

At least it should be a deal breaker. *And* you *down there,* you *don't get a vote, so get down.*

It should have cooled him off when Bast turned into a big hairy wolf.

He paced into the bath and back out.

Why isn't it a deal breaker?

Bast wasn't a wolf *all* the time. Usually he was long, tall, seductive guy.

I said down.

His cock wasn't listening.

The next morning John ran into Bast in the parking lot before roll call. He wondered if Bast had been waiting for him. John scowled at him.

"*Cher*, why the face? What's wrong?"

John whispered through clenched teeth, "I see werewolves."

"*Non. Non.* I'm not a werewolf. I'm from d' Bayou. I am loup-garou."

"You wanna know what's wrong? You killed Manolo and Sowacy."

"I didn't. They were already dead. I told you, the shadows were lodged."

"Yeah, you told me. I don't know what that means."

"It means the body was a shell. The humanity in it was gone. Manolo and Sowacy have been dead a long time. The shadow drove out the man—his spirit, his soul. Whatever you want to call it. The man was gone. Those beings were shadows walking in human bodies. Are you afraid of me now, *cher*?"

"No," John said. *Not just now. I have always been afraid of you.*

Chapter Six

Shielded in that haze that enfolds one when what is happening to him is unbearable—traumatic amnesia they called it—John was coming back to his senses. He'd been lured into a trap. Some things you just never expect. Even when it was happening, he didn't believe it. He ought to think about getting out of here.

He heard footsteps out in the alleyway. Someone was coming. And John's ass was hanging out. *Oh fuck it, why not?* This ordeal had been all about humiliation.

He did need someone to get out of this mess. *Shit.* He didn't want to be seen like this. But he wasn't going to get untied by himself.

The footsteps were right there at the door. *Oh shit.* He tried to make himself hollow. The door pushed open with a metallic creak. A wedge of light fell inward.

John lifted his head, but he couldn't really see who it was—just a backlit silhouette in the doorframe—tall, lean, with a lazy, sultry way of standing. *Shit shit shit.*

Of all people it had to be Bast.

John let his head hang. His neck hurt and he didn't want to see Bast's face when he saw this. John heard him approaching in a few swift strides.

John closed his eyes, wishing himself invisible. He was—where? He was in an abandoned building, kneeling on a ripped, stained, broken sofa. He was bent over the back of it, bleeding from his ass and half-hanging from his wrists bound with plastic twine. Another rope, strung through his bonds, had him stretched out so his arms and torso were horizontal, his head hanging down. He was too tired to lift it anymore. His arms were a solid blaze of pain.

Bast was there, his pocket knife out. He cut the rope. John dropped forward, folded over the sofa back. The screaming pain turned into an ache. All his blood rushed to his head. It was tough to breathe in this position, his nose against the back of the dusty, ratty couch. Bast circled behind him. His hands closed on the back of John's jacket. Bast pulled him back so he lay on the couch in a sideways curl, his trousers and boxers bunched around his ankles. He regarded his hands, ballooned up into unreal things. The blue and white plastic cord was almost embedded in his wrists. Bast brought his blade near, making to cut them, but John huddled protectively over his bonds. "No. 'm okay. Leave me."

Bast looked stunned. Then he was snarling around the room, lashing out at everything, punching the concrete walls and leaving bloody dents. He roared, a deep wolfish sound, full of savage fury. He hit the walls with his fists. Again. Again. Bits of concrete crumbled down. His hands ought to be broken.

John pleaded weakly, "Stop. Stop. Stop."

A strange sound came out of Bast, as if someone had stepped on a puppy. Then he demanded, his voice soft and lethal, "Who?"

John mumbled, "No." He wasn't telling.

He heard Bast exhale in a kind of cough. It sounded mystified.

Bast stalked across the room to him, all kinds of angry, then broke at the last step, falling into a kneel before him. Bast sobbed, his forehead on the couch by John's head as if he couldn't look John in the eyes, his hands up over his head in a sort of surrender. He gave a squeak, such a small sound out of such a powerful being. His body tightened in a pain shiver.

In an odd revelation, John touched the hair on top of Bast's head with backs of his swollen, bound hands. He asked, disbelieving, "Bast? Do you love me?"

Bast lifted his wet face. It was red and angry. A tear hung on the tip of his nose. He dashed it away. "What the fuck kind of question is that?"

"Do you?"

Bast's voice quivered low, a sound of wrath and defeat, "I do." He jerked with a silent sob and bowed his head again. "Damn you."

"Bast."

Bast lifted his head again. His angry, swollen eyes blinked. He snarled, "What?"

John offered his bound wrists.

Tears streamed down Bast's face and onto his lips. He drew his pocket knife and deftly tapped with the tip of blade on the just the cords. The strands of nylon opened like cruel petals.

John flexed his puffy fingers gingerly, trying to regain circulation. They stung. He inhaled on the pain and swallowed a grunt. He felt amazingly bad.

Bast had an astonishingly tender touch. The wounds on Bast's knuckles were closing before John's eyes, the bones straightening. Bast *had* broken his hands.

Bast sniffled. He dragged his jacket sleeve across his wet face. He sounded like he was trying to sound breezy. He didn't. "You know, if you want someone to beat you up, I can *do* that." A tear trickled down the side of his nose.

John tightened his brow, trying to figure out what he felt. "I don't think I do. Not really. Actually. No."

There was nothing like getting slammed to the floor to remind you which way was down—and from that, see which way was up.

Bast shut his eyes hard, as if to crush his tears back in. He asked thickly, "Who did this?"

"No," John said, still not telling.

Bast's eyes were puffing up. John could just see his black irises peering through slits. "I will find out," Bast said.

Part of John warmed to that thought. Unleashing Bast on his humiliater was a soothingly vicious thought. But John wasn't going to tell Bast who it was. That would make him as good as an accessory to murder. As outraged as he was, John hadn't lost his sense of duty as a police officer, or his humanity. "No."

He heard a rustle. It was Bast taking off his jacket. Bast blanketed it over John's bare ass and legs. Bast's body warmth—and just to be covered up—felt good.

Bast slid his arms under John's shoulders, and lifted him up just high enough to swivel himself underneath him, so Bast was sitting on the couch with John's head resting on his biceps. John felt Bast's silent sobs at his back. They gave him comfort. He felt Bast's lips brush his hair. He asked Bast, "Do you want to fuck me?"

"No," Bast mumbled, a kind of whimper.

"You do."

"Desperately. But not now."

"You could."

"I couldn't," Bast said, his accent thicker than ever, his nose stuffed.

John moved within Bast's embrace. He felt Bast's strong arms holding him, his hard torso at his back, and that really was a rigid cock poking him in the flank. "Bullshit," he told Bast.

"Oh, *cher*, that is fucking rage. You should go to the emergency room."

"I'd rather not. I mean I'd *really* rather not."

"You're bleeding, you know."

"Yeah."

"What all went up your ass?"

"I don't know." Some protective instinct inside him was blurring all the details of the whole grotesque episode.

"Foreign objects?"

"I'm fine."

"Hel-*lo?*"

"I am. I...kind of..." How to describe it? "I kind of left the building while it was happening. I don't quite remember."

"You will. It'll come back to you," Bast warned. "Hard."

"If it does, it does."

"You're looking a little shocky, John."

"Hm," John grunted, trying to figure out how he was feeling. He was feeling strange and wrong. Tremors rolled inside. "I really don't want to go to the ER."

"Then we won't go," Bast promised. John felt Bast's lips press on the top of his head and stay there.

"'kay," John said. And in a while, "What made you come here?"

"GPS locator," Bast mumbled against his scalp.

"What made you do a GPS search on me?"

"I wanted to find you."

"Why?"

"I needed to see you."

"Why?"

"I needed—" He stopped, as if struggling to hold something in. It came out. "You."

John rested his cheek on Bast's arm, wetting his cotton shirtsleeve with the flow from his eyes. He didn't even think he was crying. The tears were just sort of there. He felt the strong heartbeat of this unbelievable creature at his back, felt Bast convulse with a sob. What had to be a tear trickled down hot through John's short hair and onto his scalp. Bast tightened with a shudder like a burn pain. John felt Bast's muscles harden under the strain of holding it in. Still, to John, Bast kept only the gentlest touch.

John turned his head, his nose to Bast's biceps, his chin into the crook of Bast's elbow, his lips on Bast's shirt. He breathed in Bast's scent, and warmed against his strength. John flexed his swollen hands. He had feeling in them again. They ached. He lay a fat palm to Bast's thigh.

An odd buzzing came over him, all the way to his fingertips. He started to shake, hard. It was the strangest sensation, as if his soul returned to the empty house of his body and found it ransacked. He started to cry out loud with wild sobs.

Bast turned John toward him, and gathered him into a tight embrace, one arm around John's shoulders, the other hand behind John's thigh, his cheek against John's hair. "There it is," Bast said. John muffled his crazed cries against Bast's chest. He felt Bast's fist close on the back of his shirt. Bast held him tight through each racking sob. "I've got you, John."

I've got you.

Bast felt the blood on his fingers. Even so, he couldn't read John's mind.

I will know who did this.

John rode, strengthless and burnt out, in the passenger seat of Bast's Saab. Bast was driving him home. Nothing could make you feel more like your own grandmother than sitting on an inflatable donut at the side of a smoking hot Adonis. Bast wasn't fazed. Bast had bought him the donut, among other things, when he stopped at the drugstore on the way.

Bast walked up to his apartment with him, and sat on the bathroom floor with his back to the shower enclosure as John bathed. John could see Bast's shape through the translucent glass. John thought he would recognize that blurred shape even if he didn't know it was Bast out there.

Bast tilted his head back against the thick, tempered glass and called up, "Give me a name. I'll have him dead."

"No thank you," John called from the shower.

"You've always been a good man, John. I don't know what made me think you weren't."

John stepped out gingerly from the shower stall. He toweled himself off. Bast, now prowling his bedroom, called in, "Where do you keep your jammies?"

"Second drawer. Tee-shirt and sweats."

They came flying into the bathroom. Bast left him alone to take care of business for himself.

Bast drew back the dusky blue covers. John crawled onto the bed and flopped down on his side. Bast pulled the sheet over him and sat on the edge of the bed, his hard thigh before John's face.

John felt relaxed and mostly comfortable. He was very tired. His hands ached. His ass was sore. He hadn't bled much. He touched Bast's thigh, just to touch him. His thoughts wove in and out like wayward breezes. He murmured, "What's with the mirror?"

"What mirror, *cher*?"

"That BF thing in your office."

"For shadows," Bast said. "You can't always see them straight on, but they always show up in a mirror. Ever glimpse something in the mirror, but when you turned there was nothing there?"

John mumbled into the pillow. "I guess so. Maybe."

"A shadow was there. When the little girls look into the mirror and summon Bloody Mary, the shadows come, and the girls see them. Fortunately shadows don't like little girls. I couldn't tell you why. When they're lodged inside someone, they're obvious. I can feel them a block away. Sowacy, I could sense his for *miles*. There were so many of them. They hurt. They smell. I need to kill them. Krieg may have a dozen inside him. The day we went to see him? Between the drive to kill and all that silver pushing me back, I was sick. When they're inside someone and not lodged they don't smell, they don't—I don't know what to call it—*vibrate*. A lodged shadow makes the air sting."

"Silver. There really is something to silver?"

"I'm allergic."

"A little more than that, I think."

"A lot more than that," Bast conceded.

"Are you really a mind reader?"

"I am. Except with you. You really are a brick."

John shut his eyes. "Nothing there you want to see anyway."

Bast touched his hair. "Do you want me to stay?"

"No."

"Are you going to be all right?"

"You know what they say. What doesn't kill you…"

"Wasn't a high enough caliber."

"Yeah. I've been through worse, Bast."

"You have, but that's not helping you here."

"It means I can live through anything."

Bast brushed a kiss against his cheek in leaving.

Alone and drifting off, John knew he'd been through much worse. And he went back there, six years ago, to the day the world began to end.

He was in his apartment in Cleveland when he got the call. He had just seen Daniel two weeks earlier. It was the longest he'd ever gone without seeing his son. He hadn't got his weekend and two of his Wednesdays because Lloyd and Vanessa took Daniel on vacation with them. When the phone rang, John's heart lifted, thinking it was Daniel. It wasn't. Everything inside him crashed.

John couldn't get anyone to tell him when Daniel first got sick. He suspected Daniel wasn't feeling well even before they left on their trip. By the time they came back and took him to the hospital, he was too far gone. His kidneys had failed. John was ready to walk in front of a bus if he had any organs Daniel could use, but the surgeon couldn't operate while Daniel was riddled with infection.

Then Vanessa railed at John that he was too busy to attend the funeral.

Too busy? There was no one there John wanted to see. He was not going to see his son in a box. John was *too busy* on the day of the funeral looking alternately up the barrel of a 9 millimeter semi-auto and up the neck of a rotgut whiskey bottle, then trying to cough up his still-beating heart. He was too busy to crawl to the bathroom to try to vomit in the crapper. He just played it as it lay, and watched his sick spew across the vinyl floor along with all his tomorrows with his little boy.

Rossi, a fellow detective on the Cleveland PD and Daniel's godfather, broke into John's apartment, found him in the kitchen, cleaned up the floor, cleaned him up, made him get changed, threw his clothes in the washer, and took him for a drive. He brought John home, took his pistol and all the kitchen knives, and called him in the morning. John owed Rossi his life, though he wasn't sure he wanted it at the time.

John had Lloyd Crofton investigated for child endangerment and criminal neglect. Lloyd told him, "That's really low, John."

The investigation found nothing actionable. At a

conference between involved parties, Lloyd told Child Services, "It happened on John's weekend. The boy's father should have been watching him."

John launched himself across the table, got Lloyd by the silk tie and had him half strangled before several men pried him loose.

It was the closest to murder John had ever come.

That was until Vanessa showed up at his apartment door.

It was night. She was distraught. She didn't know where to turn. She told him no one else could possibly know what she was going through.

Okay, fine so far, but then she said she couldn't burden Lloyd with this.

John wanted badly—very very very badly—to kill her. "Please die," John said reasonably and closed the door.

John's friends in the department wanted to help. They caught Lloyd speeding. They cited his every missing taillight and ticketed him for talking on his cell phone while driving—anything they could do to rack up his points. It was the only thing they could do. John appreciated the thought.

He felt amputated. There was a giant void where the rest of his life should be. That fresh, eager presence could not possibly be gone. He felt his little guy's presence like a phantom limb. He saw Daniel everywhere.

That's where we caught our frogs for the Valley City frog jump. Daniel got stuck in the mud.

That's where we cut our own Christmas tree. The place had a live nativity scene with alpacas standing in for camels.

When jets roared overhead in an arrowhead formation on Labor Day, John wanted to call Daniel to the window. "Look, quick! It's the Blue Angels." Then he would remember Daniel wasn't there.

Anything to do with Mario and Luigi could make John mist up. Daniel wanted to be a plumber.

Then Daniel's insurance policy paid out.

John was blindsided. He never expected it. He'd started the term life insurance policy as a savings account for Daniel. John had paid into it every half year. The policy would've been worth thirty-five thousand dollars at maturity when Daniel was eighteen. It was supposed to be car or college money. John never ever expected it to actually be life insurance. The company paid out the full thirty-five thousand on Daniel's death to John as account custodian.

Money? Fuck the money.

John had to get out of that place with all its memories. He applied for an open position in the Chicago Police Department.

Six years later, the thirty-five thousand was still sitting back where he'd left it, a dead lump, in an account in Cleveland.

John got up early, thinking he'd need to take the bus this morning, but when he stepped out the front door of his apartment building he found his Chevy in its normal spot on the street. There was a red rose on the driver's seat.

Son of a bitch. John almost smiled.

John felt awkward seeing Bast in the office. He didn't say hello, because he usually didn't. But Bast brought him coffee. That raised brows, at least one pair.

Georgia asked John, "Are you two an item?"

"I—" How to answer? *Step up to the plate, John.* He wasn't going to kick Bast into the closet. And he may as well try shoving a cat into the bathtub. But he couldn't exactly say *This is my beloved*, either. "Yeah. Something's happening here."

"What it is ain't exactly clear?" Georgia guessed.

"Exactly," John said.

To everyone else, John acted the same as he always did. He refused to let himself be changed in any way by the ugly assault—outwardly, at least. His inward self would need to catch up with that program. He smiled, traded barbs with Marv, said hello to Antwan, talked sports with Thea, and traded good morning grunts with the commander. On the best of days John never wanted to put up with Chuck Wallice. John braced himself for whatever spewed out of that asshole, but Chuck scuttled into his own office and stayed there.

At lunchtime John and Bast went out for hotdogs from a cart—anything not to sit down.

John's ordeal didn't come up. John didn't want to talk about it, and Bast left it alone, but John sensed something smoldering and dangerous locked away in irons inside Bast.

John laid out ketchup on his hotdog. "So what are you? World cop? Avenging angel? I mean, why do you do it?"

"I need to. The shadows are my prey. I must seek and destroy them. I got no choice."

"Who made up that game?"

Bast lifted his shoulders and his eyebrows, mystified. "Who is the master of this show? Same one you have."

That was apparently God.

"You're Cajun," John said. "Means you're Catholic."

"Very bad Catholic. You don't get to be a loup-garou by being a good Catholic."

"You're bad for God now."

"I don't know. He don't talk to me any more than He talk to you." Bast was sounding very Cajun today.

They had picked up a small entourage of glossy-headed sky rats, who tottered hopefully after them with throaty coos.

John took a draw on his cola. "What exactly did you do to become whatever it is you are?"

Bast turned his face up toward the blue sky crisscrossed with white contrails. John couldn't see his eyes behind his sunglasses, but his smooth brow was pinched and he suddenly struck John as terribly isolated. A different breed of real lonely.

"I was bit."

"When was that?"

"A long time ago."

"You don't have a long time ago," John said. "You're only twenty-eight."

"I'm not twenty-eight."

"So when?"

"Jefferson Davis was President."

John bobbled his hotdog. "Of the *Confederacy*."

Bast nodded. "Maw Maw always told me, 'You be good or da loup-garou gonna gitchew.' It did. What I did to deserve that, I don't know. The loup-garou is supposed to have broken Lent."

"Sounds a little petty if you ask me."

"It does. They say that to scare children. If that was all there was to it, da Bayou be full of loup-garou." He'd slid back into that Black French/Spanish mush they called a language down in the swamp. "It really has to be worse than that. And I did worse. I think it must be another way of saying I offended God. I didn't believe in God at all. I guess that makes me a fallen angel. Honestly, I don't know how this game works any better than you there with the free will. I just know I'm on a mission."

"If you died would you go to heaven?"

"I don't know. And I'm so afraid to find out I'd rather—well, anything."

"How did you keep from going insane?"

"Assumes a fact not in evidence," said Bast. The corner of his eye crinkled with a wink.

John said, "I knew I was screwed even as it was coming out of my mouth. But you know what? You are a perfectly reasonable, impossible, immortal, shape-shifting hunter of evil. I'm the one whose sanity has got off-roading."

"You're not insane, John."

John swallowed his last bite of dog. He shook out his hot dog tray behind him to an eruption of flapping wings. He wadded up his trash.

"So it's really a wolf bite that does it?"

"I was bit by a man, who was loup-garou. It hurt. Not the bite. Not so much. The change, the first time. My blood turned to fire. My bones felt like they were stretching and my face pulling out of my head. And I have a hunger for darkness that can never be satisfied."

"Never?"

"Not as long as I live."

"That's apparently something like forever."

Bast didn't answer right away. "I can die if I want to."

"You obviously don't."

"I have wanted to. Badly."

Chapter Seven

John's HIV test came back negative. It had been object rape, but you never knew. It was good news.

Bast called him at home one night a couple weeks later. "Take you out to the ball game tomorrow?"

"What ball game would that be, Bast?"

"Sox versus Indians. You can't lose."

Oh. He meant a real ball game. That was a slight disappointment, but John did love baseball. He was healed and horny and wanted to be with Bast. "Sure. As long as it's not the Cubs."

"Come over for drinks afterwards, and."

Drinks and? John processed that. He said, "Should I bring a condom?" He couldn't believe that came out of his mouth. Inside him was buzzing with nerves. He never liked to show his hand, and he just had. *I want to have sex with you.* His blood raced.

"Your call."

This was not a good idea, but he knew where this was heading. He was already past the point of no return. And Bast had already declared love.

I want him.

After work, as John and Bast were walking out the door together, Bast asked, "Walk or drive?"

"Walk," John said, taking off his tie and opening his collar. "It's faster."

They stowed their IDs and stars in their jacket pockets so they could take off part of their monkey suits. Bast rolled up his shirt sleeves.

John's body hummed. Bast looked at him and asked, "You nervous?"

"No," John said, then, in a moment, "Yeah. You?"

"Of course not." Bast said. Then, "Big time."

John had brought his Aeros cap along today, and he put that on as they crossed the bridge over the Dan Ryan.

"No Indians hat?" Bast asked.

"I had one. I played for the Tribe once."

"I didn't know you made it to the majors."

"When I said once, I really meant *once*. I played part of one game. I got to witness Lastra's no hitter from the batter's box."

"Oh, no."

"Yeah. You don't never want to watch a no hitter from that position. I hit a long out to left field in the third inning and they pulled me from the rotation. I got an assist to my credit in the first inning, but they sent me back down to the minors."

"You still have your Tribe cap?"

John shook his head. "I gave it to my little guy."

The park was less than a mile from police headquarters. The new stadium backed right up to the street. John and Bast walked past all the traffic clogging West 35th.

"Kay, I already know you hate silver," John said, walking. "How 'bout garlic?"

"You have me confused with vampires."

"There are such things?"

"Hell no. Get real. Garlic just keeps you from getting a sore throat."

"Anything to the full moon? Looks like you can change any old time."

"There is definitely something to the moon. Tides.

They're stronger at the full moon. New moon too. Whenever the sun, moon, and Earth line straight up. To you it's nothing. To us, it's the rack. We're very sensitive creatures."

"I can tell," John said. "Being that full of shit would make me cranky too."

They had arrived at the stadium. John had forgotten how much energy a ball park packed. The sense of life was a physical thing—from the families, the fans, the couples, the old veterans, the school groups, the vendors hawking hats, foam fingers, popcorn, peanuts, nachos, and ice cold beee-er. The crack of the bat at practice took him back in time, to another lifetime.

Their seats were in nosebleed land. John rested his arm on the back of Bast's seat, his hand brushing Bast's back, and John saw him shiver. Bast gave him a sultry side glance from under thick lashes. Color filled his white cheeks. The pulse in his neck was visibly fast.

Bast got the hotdogs. They had mustard on them. "I wanted ketchup," John said.

Bast said, "You're in Chicago now, John. Thou shalt not put ketchup on thy hotdog. We can discuss honey or whipped cream later."

The game passed in a blurred undercurrent of anticipation. The Tribe went down but that was nothing new. John couldn't care. He wanted Bast, naked, against his body.

They funneled out of the stadium in the rivers of fans, back out to West 35th. Chicago at night was a jewel. Long ribbons of lights shone under the overpass. John took Bast's hand as they walked. They flashed each other shy, sly glances.

At the end of the bridge, a black cat hissed at them.

John pointed at the cat. "Does it know what you are?"

The cat growled an unworldly sound.

Bast wore a look of shock. The cat arched, its fur standing up along the curve of its back. Bast said hesitantly, softly, "Yeah. It must."

They walked the rest of the way in silence. John thought he could hear his own heart thudding.

When they reached the parking lot, Bast said, "About the rest of this evening's plans. I need to take a rain check."

"*What?*" For a second John thought Bast was kidding. He wasn't. "Why? Not because the cat made you, is it?"

John couldn't tell if Bast sounded brusque or panicked. He said quickly, "I got to go."

"You saw a shadow!" John guessed.

"No. I didn't."

"Then what?" *WTF. I'm getting the brush off.*

"I can't talk now," Bast said. And he was off toward his Saab with long strides.

You can't talk now? Good. 'Cause I don't want to talk to you again ever. What the fucking hell!

John was all jazzed up for tonight. He'd showered, he'd shaved, he smelled good, he'd brushed his teeth at work. Something was doing a tap dance in his stomach.

Why am I upset? It was just gonna be a fuck.

It meant a lot more than that to him.

Holy shit, this hurts.

Bast said he loved him, now he's parking him like a car? What was that about?

This shadow thing? That had to be the other side of his own split personality. *God doesn't need a hit man.*

Those tears when Bast found him—those seemed so real. John wanted them to be real. It felt good to be loved, to be cried for.

Was there one damn thing real about the man? John couldn't tell anyone about him. Bast was not going to change form in front of anyone else. John knew the first time he saw him that Bast was all wrong. John should've stayed on that course. Bast was probably working for Krieg.

That crazy lady in the parking lot a month or so ago had spotted Bast as wrong. The cat spotted him as wrong. Bast was all wrong.

John didn't believe in the mystic powers of crazy old ladies and black cats, but he didn't believe in werewolves either.

Pull it together, John. You got your little feelings hurt. Deal.

On his way home thoughts kept running 'round and 'round his head. He had to catch a bus. He'd taken a bus to work this morning, thinking he'd be riding with Bast to his house tonight. Why did Bast take him out at all tonight if he didn't want to be with him? *He took me out to ditch me here?* What was here? He couldn't think of a reason.

So he turned the problem around the other way. Bast took John out so that John wouldn't be somewhere *else*.

He's leading me off of something happening elsewhere. Where would I be if I wasn't with him?

Home.

Were Bast's cohorts planting something in John's apartment while John was at the game? Shit, that had to be it. He tried to will the bus to go faster. That hadn't worked when he was a kid, and it didn't work now.

When the bus let him off at the corner, John ran to his building, charged up the stairs, and searched his apartment for anything incriminating that could've been planted there.

He didn't know what made him think to check his home phone record. He had a flat rate plan so he never checked his logged calls, but there they were—outgoing calls he'd never made in the middle of the night, to different numbers every time. He called the numbers now. None of them was in service. Those had to be numbers to disposable phones, the kind drug dealers used.

A chill gripped his chest. Someone must've been in here rigging his phone record while John and Bast were out at the ball park. John wasn't that computer smart to know how it was done, but it had been done.

John was being set up. Bast was going to bury him with this. Those numbers were going to show up in a drug case and hang him.

Who was Bast working for? God had some weird beings working for him—seraphim and cherubim were pretty damn strange. But there were no loup-garou in the Bible. There were, however, fallen angels. They were called devils.

And devils don't work for God.

John made straight for his office after roll call. Bast followed him and started to speak. John whirled and cut him off. "Go suck a shadow."

Bast opened his mouth. Up went John's forefinger. "Save it."

"It's work related," Bast said.

"Send me an e-mail!"

"Fine!" Bast took out his phone and started texting.

"Fine!" John shut his door. He read Bast's e-mail. It detailed the latest update for the plan to catch Krieg taking a drug shipment.

Bast sat in a borrowed car. His old Saab with its quirky shape was too recognizable, and this wasn't a departmental stakeout. It was his. He parked at the corner of the brownstone apartment building. He hoped he wasn't going to see anything tonight.

Two hours past midnight the outer door of the brownstone opened. *There. There he goes.*

John Hamdon climbed into his Chevy. Bast tailed him at a distance. He thought John might've made him, so Bast let him get ahead and out of sight. Bast was afraid he already knew where John was going. After an hour, Bast let himself catch up with John again, just in time to see John's car turn off the road and drive through Krieg's open gates. The gates closed behind him.

Bast drove on past for several miles. He had to pull over to the side of the road. He rested his head on the wheel and took in shuddering breaths, his nose thick, his eyes stinging. He gripped and re-gripped the wheel, then beat on it with his fists. He charted a different route home, rolled up the windows, and howled in the car.

John dragged into the office. He'd slept a solid eight hours and it felt like none. It made him surly, and he was in no mood to see Bast, ever.

"I need you to see something." Bast said.

John squinted at him. "What?"

"I need you to tell me what you think."

"Where is it?" John said, curt.

"Off site."

"Why me?"

"Because you've seen Krieg."

John couldn't let his anger at Bast get in the way of investigating a case. And he couldn't tell him, *I'm not going with you, you're a devil.* That sounded deranged in the morning light. He said, "Lemme get more coffee."

In the break room John pulled out his cell phone, dialed his voice mail, and slipped the phone in his breast pocket, recording. His voice mail was set up to take extremely long messages. He wanted a recording of whatever happened on this trip.

He grabbed a cup of coffee and joined Bast. "I'm ready."

Bast drove a city car out to the county forest preserve. If it had been the Saab, John wasn't getting in.

Bast didn't drive in through one of the park entrances. He pulled off the road onto a grassy shoulder, checked the GPS coordinates, got out of the car, and led the way into the woods. They had to be close to Sag Quarries.

The caffeine kicked in as John was high stepping over thorns and ducking under tree boughs and pulling burrs off his blazer. It occurred to him that this would be a good place to dump a body. *Hope it's not mine.* He thought he was being funny.

The wind picked up. The poplar leaves pattered wild applause, making it sound like it was raining.

They came to a small clearing where the sun penetrated the forest canopy. Bast turned around and told him, "John Hamdon is dead."

"What?" John Hamdon said.

"John Hamdon died on Bellus Road on the nineteenth of April. You are a shadow."

"And you are a dick," John said back.

"I was chasing a shadow when I got hit by a car. I couldn't pick the trail back up again. I couldn't understand how it could get that far ahead of me. It didn't. I left it back on the road. It hit me with its car."

"Are you sniffing something from the evidence locker?"

"A shadow entered John Hamdon. He hit me with his car. Then the shadow killed him."

John pressed his finger to the bridge of his own nose. "Look at me. Focus here, Bast. I'm not dead."

"You've been looking for a traitor in our section who is leaking secrets to Krieg's organization. If you've looked everywhere and you're coming up empty handed, look inside yourself. You're it."

"Where the wild fuck are you getting this from?"

"That's why Krieg laughed when I asked him who he had in our organization. The guy Krieg has was standing right next to me. I brought Krieg's own snitch with me to talk to him!"

"Bast, this is nuts even for you. Please drop it now."

"Remember when I e-mailed you about a shipment yesterday? You turned around and passed that information to Krieg."

"I didn't. If he found out, it wasn't from me. Someone else had to tell him."

"*Who* else? *I made it up*! It was all shit!" Bast's voice cracked. He sounded near crying. "I told it to you and only to you. But the information got to Krieg and he swallowed it—because it came from his trusty shadow-infested snitch."

"I didn't tell him squat!"

"You drove to Krieg's place last night. Krieg acted on the crap you told him. There will be people seriously upset with Krieg today. He's going to need to find a new house. I need to catch him on moving day."

John knew Bast wasn't talking about a house house. He was talking about a living human body as a place for a shadow to live.

John's anger caved into doubt, then into a deep oh shit, wondering if it was true. A tremor started in his hands. He dropped his coffee cup. He was tired as if he hadn't slept at all. Because he *hadn't* slept.

I didn't do that. I couldn't.

Anytime he'd heard information on how the Bureau was going to catch Krieg, John was dragging the next day. *I've been walking.*

Bast said, "And then there's you."

"What are you going to do to me?"

"Like to fuck you blind. But you're not John. This is a real problem."

"You THINK?"

"I'm afraid I need to kill you, but you're not really John. John is dead. You're so like John. This is hard. I'm sorry." Bast drew a weapon, not police issue. And Lord almighty, Bast had a silencer.

John forced his voice into a congenial tone, like talking to a hop head, "Bast, get back in your lane. You're drifting over the double yellows."

"You won't feel much." Bast leveled the gun at his head. "Steady."

Screw congeniality. "Are you fucking insane!"

"Stay still. Face me. You can close your eyes, but open your mouth. You shouldn't feel much."

John saw black. Between rage and fear, he yelled, "Get fucking fucked!" And he dropped to the ground, drawing his 9 mil. He emptied the clip into Bast—like shooting himself in the gut.

Bast recoiled from the impacts but kept hold of his own pistol, stumbling once, and advanced like a movie zombie.

John threw his gun at Bast, missed, and scrambled to turn and run. Something—two paws of a wolf—hammered down on his back and he was thrown forward.

He landed face down in the leaf litter and acorns. He spat dirt and ants—still alive, with a wolf on top of him, its heavy paws finding footing on his back, gathering its center and launching off him. Air left John's pressed lungs with an ooof. The exhalation from his mouth was black.

From one eye he barely glimpsed the gray-black wolf flying over his head, lunging after the darkness.

The darkness was real. It was a moving black mass, weirdly flat and twisting, changing shape, expanding and contracting like a diseased lung. And Bast, the wolf, was still alive with a load of metal in his chest and gut. The wolf inhaled the writhing darkness. The shadow convulsed, snapping like a black flag. Its ragged edges clawed at the air, fighting, tearing. The wolf stood straight up, still trying to draw it all in. He tottered backwards.

Bast, a man again, fell to the ground, swearing out light ash-gray smoke. He crawled back to his coat and fumbled for a pocket. He flipped something at John. "Keep this on you in case it comes back."

This was a cigarette lighter. John wasn't sure which question to ask first. *What the hell is this for? What the hell was that?* or *What the fuck are you?*

Bast stood up, took one running step, stumbled, and fell forward, his hands skidding through brown leaves and light green moss. "Son of a bitch. You got me in the spine." He spat up a bullet and shook like a dog, his wounds closing before John's eyes. Bast, in obvious pain, complained loudly, "Oh, bugger bugger buggest."

John snarled at him, at a complete loss for anything rational to say. "Bugger? You're not British. Where do you get off saying bugger, *cher?*"

"Has a better rhythm than fuck, *n'est pas?* Ow!"

"I think you should shut up."

"And I think you should fuck me—" Bast broke off in a sudden roar. He crouched, with his long arms looped around his narrow waist. He paused for an apparent stab of pain. "Screw." He fell forward, then looked up at John from hand and knees, surprised and wounded. "You *shot* me."

His brain overloaded, John said dully, "You were

trying to kill me."

"If I wanted to kill you, you'd be dead. And by the way, I never give warnings or make speeches to my targets. I just do 'em. *Ow.*" He leaned over, head down, and hawked up another bullet. He lay all the way forward, his chin resting on the ground. He panted through his nose.

The very back of John's mind was registering that he was a pretty good shot, and that Bast had a superb ass, but Bast's words were catching up. "Comes back? What do you mean in case *it* comes *back?*"

"I didn't get it all. There were two." Puffs of air from his words moved a dried leaf in front of his mouth.

"Two what? What the hell was that?" John didn't mean it as a real question but Bast answered.

"Hell," he said. "I had to scare it out of you. You had shadows in you."

"You might have told me!" *And then I would think you were a raving jackshit, when I'm actually the raving jackshit having hallucinations.*

Bast rolled over onto his back in the brown leaves and white wildflowers. And wasn't that a picture. He was a young woodland god, his hair in disarray, his cock standing at half staff from his pubic hair, his white skin closing over the sharply defined muscles of his abdomen. Bast wiped the blood off his now-smooth belly with the side of his hand, his eyes directed up to the sky.

He stood up, shaking leaves and lichen from his hair. "The only way to get them out of you was to make them think you were dying. You had to sell it for me. They knew if they stayed inside you while you died, they would die too. It would have been simpler and safer just to choke you to death while you didn't expect it and make sure I got them. You would be a lot deader, though. It was much, much trickier making them believe I was about to kill you." He inspected the last traces of his wounds in his midsection. "I guess I did all right."

"Oh, you were stellar." John hauled back a fist and cracked Bast across the jaw.

Bast went down again. He lifted himself up on his forearms, his hair hanging forward, saliva dripping from his lips, as he waited for his jaw to mend.

John growled, "Get your pants on." His insides were sparking. It felt like he'd swallowed a downed power line.

Bast opened and shut his mouth experimentally. His jaw was back in place. He said, "'Sorry for shooting you, Bast. Are you going to live, Bast? Thank you for taking the trouble to separate the bad shit out of me instead of throwing out the cop with the bath water, Bast.'"

"I'm not thanking you for that," John said. His voice vibrated. "Do you know what it's like to look up the barrel of one of those when you can *really die*?" He threw Bast's pants on him. They were black, so John felt rather than saw the blood on them.

Bast rose to a crouch, but didn't stand up. John's eyes went to the indentations in Bast's cheeks where the hard cords of his ass knit together. The exit wounds had vanished from his artistically muscled back. Bast was picking through the leaf bits, twigs, and moss for something.

In the blink of an eye—and John hadn't thought he'd blinked—Bast was a wolf again, sniffing and scratching at the forest floor.

John suddenly realized what Bast was looking for. *My brass.*

The wolf nosed a spot, John picked up the bullet, then another, then a casing.

"Nine and nine. That's all of them," John said at last. He jingled them in his hand. They were still warm.

Bast, the man, was pulling on his trousers.

John picked up Bast's bloody shirt. His fingers went

through the bullet holes. "You're a Terminator."

"Pretty much."

"Don't those magic clothes close up too? They do on TV."

"That's why they call it fantasy, John. We need to get out of here."

Yeah. There had been gunshots. *Before someone calls the cops.*

"Who are you calling?" Bast asked.

John had pulled his cell phone from his pocket. "I gotta delete my voice mail. I'm recording."

"You ass," Bast said.

"You threatened to kill me!"

"You shot me!"

Bast wadded up his bloody shirt and jacket. He slung his holster over one bare shoulder. He looked like a wet dream, hard, a little leaner than John thought he was. Bast's trousers looked loose. John thought it was a trick of the forest light, but Bast said, "I'm starving. Feed me."

John blinked at him. "You *do* look thin."

"Regenerating takes it out of me."

"What happens if you don't eat?"

"I waste away to bones." He tossed John the keys to the car. "You drive. Find a drive through. Fast food. Anywhere. Let's go." He sounded literally starving.

"You gonna bite me?" John asked.

"Not today, *cher*. The moon is full."

John couldn't see it. The moon was on the night-side of the world. In Perth, Australia there were wolves howling at the full moon. "Isn't that when you do your biting?"

"I'll bite anytime. Under the full moon is the only time the bite is more than a bite. All of us were made under the full moon. A bite as man or beast—it don't matter. If I bite you under this moon, you're part of the club."

John put the pedal down to get to a burger joint fast.

He didn't ask anymore questions until Bast was wolfing down half pounders.

"I was working for Krieg?" John asked in sick disbelief.

"Not *you*, John Hamdon. You were the vehicle for the shadows."

Vehicle? "Just great. I'm a Buick."

"The shadows couldn't control you while you were awake, but they were watching me. You were delivering messages when you were asleep. Didn't you notice you were putting miles on your odometer overnight?"

John hadn't been putting on miles at all. "It stopped working after the accident."

"Turn here." Bast pointed suddenly. "Park."

John made the turn. As he parallel parked he said, "Full moon. Is that why you changed into a wolf today? You're going premenstrual on me."

Bast curled a lip at him. John quickly passed him his own French fries.

Bast said, "The urge is stronger. All urges are stronger."

"All?"

"I want you." Bast's thick lashes hung heavy over his deep dark eyes, smoldering with hunger.

"As in sex or biting? If it's sex, I'm okay with that." In fact he was hornier than he'd been in a long, long time.

"I'm afraid I'll bite you having sex."

"How afraid?"

"Get out of the car."

Chapter Eight

John took the bus home. He cleaned and reloaded his weapon, brushed all the leaf bits off his jacket and trousers, fixed his tie, and washed his hands. He took a bus back to the office.

He didn't see Bast again that day. It was Friday. He wouldn't see Bast again until Monday at work. He didn't even have Bast's personal phone number to talk to him. And he missed him.

He spent the night awake in his half-empty bed, with that useless second pillow, a scent missing from it. He'd never known what it was like to want someone so much it hurt, and not just because his balls were blue. He felt that tightness in the chest that made it hurt to breathe, and that waffle in the midriff because he just didn't want to fuck this up.

Saturday night rolled around. John hadn't seen Bast. John pictured him out somewhere howling at the moon.

Then his intercom buzzer sounded late in the night. John was still awake, restless. His body shifted into high gear. He glanced out the window. The moon was up. It looked just a bit less than fully round. He touched the intercom button. "Hamdon."

The voice through the speaker was Bast's. "Hi. I just ran away from a party. Are you alone? Are you busy? Can I come in?"

John buzzed the downstairs door open. But Bast's voice came through the speaker again, "Just a minute. I gotta pay the taxi."

John waited for Bast to buzz again, then pressed the button to let him in. John barely heard him climbing the stairs. Bast had a light tread.

John opened his apartment door. "Are you drunk?"

Bast walked in, merrily disheveled and smelling of rum. He talked faster than usual. "No. Someone spilled that on me. I only drink when I don't need my brain."

"What do you need your brain for here?" John closed the door.

"*You're* here," Bast said. He seized John's head and planted a firm kiss on his lips. Bast didn't taste of alcohol. But his eyes had a glassy look to them.

"What am I going to do to you?" John asked.

"That's the question, isn't it?" Bast said, sounding like he was trying to be carefree, but it came out tense. "I don't have experience."

John drew his chin back. "*You* don't? You're screwing with me."

"I have never made love."

"I don't believe that."

"I think I said what I meant. Sex—I can do that several ways. Love. That's a new one. I want you more than I should. This means more than it should. Maybe I should have a drink. What you got?"

"No." John took Bast's face in his hands and looked into his wide eyes. Bast was honest to God afraid. John was the rookie here, and he'd never felt so sure of himself. This felt entirely right.

He hadn't been aware of the shadows inside him until they were gone. He just knew he'd been in a tailspin ever since he crashed into Bast. Now the shadows were gone, and he was awake, alive, back in control, and he knew what he wanted.

He pressed a kiss to Bast's lips, softly. It was almost sweet, but with a slow heat, moving his mouth across

Bast's yielding lips. Bast's eyelids drooped languorously. His eyes were completely shut when John drew away.

John fished a condom from his pocket. He'd been carrying it around for a while now. "Do we need this?"

"No," Bast said.

"I guess wolfmen don't get HIV." John tossed the condom aside.

"I don't know if we do or not. I got tested."

John started to say something, remembered that he was talking to a mind reader, so he said something else. "You know what I'm thinking. You know what I want."

"Not at the moment, no," Bast said. He kept dropping his gaze, then hauling it back up to look John in the eyes. "When it comes to that I'm as blind as anyone. No one can read da heart. And in love I can get as scared as anyone."

"Are you scared?"

"Terrified."

John put his arms around Bast, pulling him in to a tight embrace. "Don't be afraid of me." He kissed Bast deeply. He felt hunger and longing in Bast's return kiss. John plunged his tongue into Bast's mouth, and Bast responded in kind. Bast's breaths puffed against his face steamy and fast. A sound in Bast's throat may have been pleasure or fear or both.

John let his hands rove slowly over Bast's lean body, feeling his hard sinews through his shirt. Bast's arms surrounded him. His body moved against John's. John took hold of one cheek and pulled Bast in firmly against him, full length, hard cock pressed against hard cock. Bast lifted a leg to hook around John's ass. They teetered and stepped apart to catch their balance.

John took Bast's hand and led him into the bedroom.

It was a spare, modern space decorated with light-colored wood and trim lines. There were wood blinds over the windows, a jute carpet underfoot, and a sage green comforter on the bed. The last time Bast had been in here, John was in distress. Now the place suddenly looked magical.

Bast stepped ahead and rolled onto the bed, ending face up. John climbed onto the mattress and put one arm across Bast's body, his weight on his hand. He looked down on Bast's face. This was not a position he ever expected them to be in—with Bast on his back. In wolves that was a submissive posture.

The expression on Bast's face—John had seen that look before. On virgins. John was pretty sure Bast wasn't one of those.

Bast looked apprehensive, and somehow soft. He seemed very young now, but then everyone looks younger on his back. John moved a dark lock off Bast's brow with the back of his finger. "Bast? Are you a girl?"

Bast blinked up at him. "Well, apparently, that depends."

"On?"

"On who I'm with, you dick."

John guessed Bast was used to being an alpha. He'd run into a stronger alpha. His surrender was grudgingly given. "You really *are* afraid of me," John said.

"No. Not really. I might…possibly…maybe…" Bast's voice drizzled away. "Am."

Bast had always struck him as beautiful. John always pushed the notion out of his head every time it crossed his mind. He let himself see it now.

Bast's exotic eyes were nearly black and striking against his white skin. The dark fringe of his lashes lowered shyly then lifted again to return John's gaze frankly. It was late, and there was a haze of downy beard shadow along Bast's jaw that made him look roguish. John traced the line of it with his finger. Bast's mouth was seductive, with a slight bow curve to his upper lip over his full lower lip that wanted kissing. His pulse was visible—moving very quick—in his long white throat. John saw moisture on Bast's lips and a tremor in his narrow nostrils.

John could scarcely believe he had Bast on his back and trembling. John felt a warm anticipation, aroused, and happier than he could remember. He smiled down at Bast's face. "You ever picture this?"

"I've always wanted to surrender. I never met anyone I could surrender to."

"What do you want from me?" John asked.

"Love?" Bast said like a suggestion. "Is it too much to ask?"

John hesitated.

"It is, isn't it?" Bast said.

"No. I was just wondering if I have it to give. Apparently I do." He'd thought it was too soon to know. But it wasn't. There was no need for dithering and dicking around when he was certain. *When you know, you know*. His head was clear of shadows and now he knew. "I love you, René Bast."

Bast's body was ringing the perfect chord. The words he'd heard before—many times. He'd never wanted them before. Finally he got to hear them from the man who was meant to say them. Bast wanted John Hamdon, heart, mind, sex, and soul. He wanted *that* cock, sight unseen. He hadn't looked when he'd come upon John ravaged in the abandoned building. It seemed an intrusion at the time. And he didn't even care what John's cock looked like now, because it belonged to that body, that mind, that soul, that strong, stubborn, courageous, amazing being. Only John's touch would do, only John's heartbeat next to his.

John was awfully young, just thirty-two, but he'd taken some hits. He had lived. He had died inside. And still he pushed on, head up. Because of his scars—inside and out—Bast could submit to this man.

Bast had always been seeking relief, and never getting more than that. In the past he was just getting rid of this piece of wood. No one ever touched him. He felt no more for his many partners than he cared what the mattress he humped felt or thought. This time he cared. And felt more naked than he'd ever been.

John was unbuttoning Bast's shirt, slowly, button by slow button, parting his shirt front. It made Bast shiver in anticipation. John asked, "I know there's different ways to do this. What am I doing here?"

"Anything and everything you want to do to me, I promise to be thrilled out of my mind. Just get your cock inside me."

"I was hoping you'd say that. Just don't turn into a wolf."

"No," Bast promised.

"Do we need lubricant?"

"You really did think you were straight, didn't you?" Bast arched up on the mattress to pull a tube from his hip pocket.

John caressed Bast's side. Bast was trembling. John unfastened the snap of Bast's black jeans and unzipped his fly. He reached inside, surprised and thrilled not to feel a thong, just springy hair and a smooth erect cock, moist at the tip.

Bast was wide eyed as John knelt up and pulled off his own shirt. Bast arched up again to pull his jeans down and kick them off. He had long, long, sleekly muscled legs.

John stepped off the bed and pushed down his own trousers. He got one foot free, did the one-legged hop to get the other foot free, then climbed back onto the bed. He pushed one knee then the other between Bast's legs and hand-walked himself forward to kiss Bast's mouth, his neck, his shoulder. Bast's arms surrounded him and pulled him down flush to him, body to body, sex to sex, his hips thrusting. John met him thrust for thrust, the feeling beyond any dream he'd ever had. It was all new and incredible as if he'd reinvented sex. He was way too hot, and he wasn't going to last. He pushed himself back up and ordered, "Roll over."

Bast was over as fast as saying it. John covered him, his teeth on the back of Bast's shoulder, his cock riding in the cleft between Bast's splendidly hard buttocks. He knelt back and dragged his tongue up the length of Bast's spine, from his ass to the base of his skull.

Bast's back rounded as he drew his knees up under himself. John urgently patted around on the sheets for whatever the hell he'd done with the lube. Bast found the tube and hastily passed it back behind him. John slicked his own cock and the channel between Bast's buttocks. His head filled with cinnamon scent.

His cock touched Bast's sweet ass in a shimmering moment. A low moan sounded from inside Bast's throat. John nestled his hard sex inside the smooth furrow between Bast's hard cheeks, and he slid back and forth, slowly at first, pleasure building in delicious agony. He pressed his lips to Bast's heated back. His lips moved against his damp skin. "Are you ready?"

"Been," Bast mumbled, his head bowed to the mattress.

With more restraint than he felt, John carefully pushed inside the tight hole, shuddering with the pleasure, intense as a burn, but shatteringly sweet. Bast's flesh surrounded him, held him. John gave a broken groan of absolute wonder. He penetrated Bast's ass up to his own balls and carefully withdrew and pushed again. "Oh my God, René."

"You can go harder," Bast breathed.

"I don't want to hurt you." John was straining not to. He'd broken a hot sweat.

"Do it."

John drove into heat and splendor. He gripped Bast's narrow hips and thrust faster and faster.

He felt a pulsing wave surround his plunging cock, and he lost control. His balls tightened. He came in blazing surges of ecstasy, every fiber of his body alive and exulting. Bast uttered a sound between a snarl and a cry. John felt tension ripple within Bast's body. Bast was coming too. Another tremor of redoubled pleasure gripped John, and he came some more, his body washed with unimaginable bliss.

At the last flare and shiver, Bast lowered his head to rest his brow on his forearms. He panted, speaking in mumbled French. John knelt there, his cock inside Bast, savoring a last spasm. With his hands John worshipped Bast's beautiful ass and his sweaty sides. He bent forward and kissed Bast's back. His skin tasted salty. At last, John withdrew and dropped onto the bed at Bast's side.

Bast stretched out full length, purring.

John rolled onto his side, meaning to take Bast into his arms. He was horrified to see a slight red tint on his own cock. "I hurt you."

"I'm indestructible," Bast mumbled into the pillow.

John put his arm across Bast. "I didn't want to hurt you."

"*I* wanted it," Bast said.

"Do you like pain?"

"Some."

Bast quarter-turned to face John and sidled closer,

nestled against his chest. John lifted his left arm to let Bast slide his right arm underneath it and circle John's chest. They both jockeyed for where to put their other arms.

John kissed Bast alongside his nose. "Do we need a stop word?" John asked. "In case I go too far? I can't tell."

"How about 'stop?'" Bast said.

"Stop?" John echoed.

Bast shrugged within John's embrace. "It's not imaginative but it's easy to remember."

"It's also easy to blurt when you don't mean it," John said.

"Then how about, 'John, please stop, I really mean it.'"

"I like it," John said. Plain talk, straight to the heart. This wasn't a game.

When Bast got passionate, his accent was impenetrable. They didn't need words anyway. Bast had been talking in Cajun while they fucked.

"Why did you keep telling me to shut the door?" John asked.

Bast's face went blank for a second, then he laughed. "*Je t'adore! Je t'adore!*"

"What door?"

"I adore you, you ass."

"Is that what you said?"

Bast's cheek moved against the pillow with his nod. "Except I didn't call you an ass."

"I have a hard enough time understanding you when you think you're speaking English." John gave him a gentle kiss. "By the way, I'm sorry I shot you."

Bast smiled. He looked young and vulnerable, naked, with his hair spread on the pillow.

John let his own rough fingers trace the interplay

of hard muscles in Bast's elegantly sculpted shoulder. "René?"

"Hm?"

"Shut the door."

Bast's gaze shifted over John's face, the sharp planes in it, hard, determined. Bast wanted to memorize every detail of John as he was right now. Bast needed to hold the moment. John was aging, and Bast wasn't.

John's butch hair had been brown-blond when Bast first met him. It was sun scorched, copper gold now. His face was a hard kind of handsome with strong features. There was a pale mask around his eyes from wearing sunglasses. When John had sunglasses on, he looked like he should be chasing Arnold Schwarzenegger with an M72 LAW's rocket launcher.

Bast leaned over John, groping at his back.

"What you doing back there?" John asked lazily, his head pillowed on one arm. His bulky biceps couldn't be a comfortable pillow.

"You've been shot," Bast said.

John grunted affirmative. Bast gave a warm shiver, feeling John's rough hand gliding across his skin.

A true blue hard man, John kept taking hits and he got up every time. The shot hadn't been a Hollywood shot—one of those rounds through the shoulder you saw in every other cop show. This round had gone through John's gut and just missed his spine as it went out the other side. The surgeon's cut was in the front. He or she had had been neat. The small starburst exit wound scar was on John's back.

That had to be an armor piercing round—makes for a neat hole in a man. John was lucky. As lucky as a man could be, getting shot.

John reached across him for the nightstand. Bast watched the movement of the muscles in his side and under his powerful arm. The tuft of brown hair in the pit was raw, male, and sexy. John picked up something. "This." Bast saw what he had. The lighter Bast had flipped to him in the forest. "You gave this to me."

"Yes," Bast said. "In case of shadows."

"You didn't tell me what to do with it."

Bast made a face, inwardly calling himself an idiot. He said seriously, "If you think you see a shadow, hold it in front of your face like you're lighting a cigarette. Shadows don't like fire."

John put the lighter back on the nightstand, and glanced at the clock. He fell back on the bed with a groan. "I'm going to be a wreck in the morning—"

Bast moved to get up.

John held him down with a warm heavy arm. "—and I don't give a flying ferret."

Bast said reluctantly, "I should go."

"Stay," John said.

Bast didn't want to go. He felt warm and snug under John's arm. "I need clothes." The clothes he'd worn here weren't work appropriate and they smelled rummy.

"You didn't think this through, did you?" John said.

"I was afraid to get my hopes too high. I need a shower."

"Take it here."

"It'll take longer if I shower here. You know that."

John rolled up and off the bed, and took Bast by the hand. "Then let's get started."

Bast and John stood together under the warm water, holding each other, forgetting they were supposed to be washing. Bast ran his hands over John's broad, hard-muscled back. He felt John's lips, hot on his neck. He felt John's cock roll up the inside his thigh, hardening. Bast licked John's broad shoulder. John had a boxer's shoulders, a thick cap of powerful muscle padding over the joint there. Bast traced John's sternum with his tongue, down his navel, and below the tan line to white skin. Bast slid his hands behind John's thickly corded thighs. He held his breath under the water stream, and sucked John's stiffening cock until John was grunting, grasping at Bast's hair, and coming in Bast's mouth.

"Sorry," John mumbled after he came down a little from his dizzy peak.

"Don't be an ass," Bast said and rinsed his face under the shower spray.

"Then how about 'thank you?'"

"You're welcome," Bast said.

Bast stepped out of the shower first. He set a drinking glass precariously on the very edge of the countertop, grabbed a towel, and went out to John's bedroom to dry off.

In a moment, he heard breaking glass and John's voice. "Damn it."

Bast looked in. John was picking up pieces of broken glass. He was being careful, but he'd cut his finger anyway. *Sorry about that, John.*

"Don't step. Let me get this," Bast said. He dragged the side of his hand across the wet floor to get all the pieces. He didn't care if he got cut, and he found all the tiny invisible bits. He put the shards into the trash and washed his hands. His shallow cuts were all healed by the time he dried his hands. The towel came away clean. He reached for John's hand. "Let me see that."

John was toweling himself off. "It's nothing."

Bast took John's cut finger into his mouth, softly sucking—and he read John's mind.

Bast already thought he knew the name of his prey, but John had a world class poker face, so Bast hadn't been completely sure before this moment.

When Bast was going to murder a man, he wanted to be dead certain.

Monday morning before roll call, John had a hard time keeping contact between his shoe soles and the floor. He was flying.

Georgia Grover took one look at him and broke a huge smile. "John. You dog, you." She patted his arm. "Good for you."

Bast made it to the office just in time for roll call. He had the look of a cat lying in a mess of yellow feathers.

John and Bast ate lunch out, together, their ankles touching under the table at the restaurant.

"Come over after work?" John asked.

"I have something to attend," Bast said.

John had *not* expected that answer. He put down his fork. "Screw it, Bast. Don't tell me I have another shadow in me."

"No. You're good. There's something I need to do."

As they were walking out of the restaurant, John caught Bast between the inner and outer doors. He turned Bast around, took his face, and kissed him on the mouth, soulful and deep. He drew back and asked, "Still have something to do?"

Bast looked torn. "Yes," he said. "It's important."

***

Chuck Wallice looked over his shoulder at his companion. "You got my back, right?"

"Oh, yeah."

It was three o'clock in the morning. Some bozo was mashing on John's buzzer. John lugged himself to his feet, trudged to the door, and pressed the intercom button. "Who is it?" he snarled, expecting some drunk. And he was right.

"Your girlfriend. I'm pregnant."

John buzzed Bast in. Unsteady footsteps thumped up the stairs, and Bast spilled into John's apartment, aromatic. This time he really was drunk—as a six-pack of skunks. He put his hands to John's face, gazed deep into his eyes, and said, "Windows are the eyes of the soul."

"That makes no sense whatsoever."

"It does when you're drunk."

"Were you driving drunk?"

"I broke the law. Show me no mercy."

John herded Bast—Bast's long arms and legs had turned him into a herd—into the bedroom. Bast missed the bed and crumpled to the floor. "Get up," John said.

"I think I am," Bast said, lying face up on the floor, his cock tenting his trousers.

"I'm not having sex with a drunk," John said.

"Please," Bast said, his voice lucid and quietly urgent. "I need you now."

John crawled over him on hands and knees and looked down into Bast's eyes.

The windows of his soul were wide open.

John gave him a kiss that was supposed to be tender, and it started that way, but it caught fire. It was a fierce, devouring kiss, and Bast clung to him in passionate need, letting go only long enough for them to get their trousers off. Then John was on him again, his thick cock rubbing against Bast's long erection, slick with precome.

John got his hands under Bast and lifted his ass off the floor. Bast brought his knees up to hug John's body between his hard thighs, his anus beckoning right at John's rigid eager cock.

"René—" John was about to say something about him not being wet enough.

"I'm way ahead of you. Bring it," Bast said.

And John, aroused past any restraint, pushed his cock through that tight hot gate, in and out, sliding easily. He smelled cinnamon.

Bast had a change of clothes in his car. In the morning John and he drove in to headquarters together. For as drunk as Bast had been last night, he should've been hammered this morning. Bast was as chipper and happy as larks sounded like they were.

"You should have called me to come get you last night," John said at the wheel of Bast's Saab. "That was dumb, driving like that."

"I was in complete command and control until I got to your door, *cher*. Then I didn't want to be in control anymore."

John drove in silence for a few moments. Then he said, "You need to tell me where to get that cinnamon stuff."

He heard the glove box opening. Then Bast was slipping a tube into John's breast pocket.

Getting coffee before roll call, John was on a high glide.

Meyers poked his head into the break room. "Where's Chuck?" Chuck Wallice was usually the first one here. "Does anyone know where Chucky is?"

"Don't care," John growled low. Then, on a sudden dark thought, he looked around for Bast.

Bast was rummaging through drawers. His face lifted. "Does anyone know where the coffee filters are?"

Chapter Nine

For the second day in a row, Chuck Wallice was a no-show.

At lunchtime the commander stepped into the break room. He had an announcement. "I have bad news. The details of this are not for the public. I regret to report the death of Detective Chuck Wallice."

Amid rustles, stirrings, and murmurs, John held back from saying anything. He hoped Chuck died ugly.

The commander reported that Chuck Wallice had choked to death on a dildo while bound and cuffed and wearing the whole leather kink rig.

John forgot to swallow. He coughed. Thea Pittman-Jones gave him a thump on the back.

"*Chucky?*" Marv Meyers said. "He's the last guy I'd ever peg for that type. I'd've thought an S but never an M."

"You just never know, do you?" Antwan said, waiting for the microwave to ding.

"He *died?*" It wasn't really a question. Georgia was having trouble believing it. "I thought S and M was consensual."

The commander said somberly, "The consent is in question. Coroner is saying it took Detective Wallice hours to die. He suffered."

Georgia said hopefully, "Well, that means he died happy, doesn't it?"

"I will let you know about funeral arrangements when I know," the commander said and left the break room.

"I guess it's tough to say your safe word with a woodie down your throat," Antwan said.

"I guess," Georgia said.

"Safe word?" Meyers asked.

Thea said, "It's a signal. Something you say instead of No or Stop to say No or Stop."

Georgia added, "In S and M 'no' doesn't mean 'no' and 'stop' doesn't mean 'stop.' So they pick something else they won't say by accident. Like Fledermaus or rutabaga."

"And just how do you all know this?" Meyers let his stirring stick seesaw from one to the other to the other.

"Hel-LO. Two years on vice?" said Antwan, bringing his steaming lunch to the table.

"I watch CSI," Georgia said.

"I read a lot," Thea said.

As the news buzzed through the offices, John noticed that absolutely no one was grieving.

Bast wasn't weighing in. He wasn't even at the table. He was watching the little TV on the other side of the break room. A baseball game was on. Bast lounged almost horizontal in a chair, one long leg hooked over the armrest of another chair. Meyers bounced a wadded paper napkin off his head. "Hey N'Orleans. Nothing to add?"

Bast—always good for an evil comment—was staying oddly quiet. He gestured with a kernel of popcorn at the TV screen. "I think the Cubbies might actually win this game."

At the end of the work day the commander asked his detectives to stay for a meeting. "New case. Chuck Wallice. I don't have to tell you this is one of our own. *Stop sniggering!*"

Chasing Shadows

They did their best, but devolved fast, their faces contorted, trying hard not to grin or make any sound like a laugh. They only got worse and worse. John was trying to swallow his upper lip. Meyers had his hand to his mouth. Antwan's lips were writhing and trembling. For a moment Antwan lost it, flashed a blinding white smile, and immediately squelched it. Thea looked to be trying hard not to laugh. She had tears running down her cheeks, not from grief. Bast slouched way down, his arms crossed, staying out of it.

The commander thundered, "Detective Bast! You take this one."

Bast sat bolt upright. "*Moi? Mai non!*"

"*Problem*, Detective?" The commander's voice was menacing.

Bast looked to be grasping at the air for an excuse, any excuse. He sputtered, "But—But *I did it!*"

The commander was not amused. "It's your case," he said and dismissed the rest of them, disgusted.

Bast walked up to accept the case folder, not looking the commander in the eyes. Bast felt his mouth getting wiggly. "Do this right, Detective Bast. By the book. If you dare smile I will shoot you."

Mouth twitching, his voice a little breathy, on the verge of losing it, Bast said, "Yessir. I'll do my damndest."

The commander sighed, and let his head hang in defeat. He spoke into his own broad chest. "Chucky really was a dillweed, wasn't he?"

John took the bus home, got changed out of his work clothes, then drove to Bast's house. He let himself in with the key Bast had given him. He dropped his bag inside the door. He was spending the night.

"Bast?" John said, like a question.

"John?" Bast said, standing, backlit, in the bedroom doorway.

John couldn't see his face, only a dark silhouette. "Was Chuck a shadow?"

"No."

No. It was several moments before John could bring himself to speak again. "You tortured and murdered a man."

"Yes."

Bast had just quietly admitted to first degree premeditated murder. Of a cop.

At first John had premeditated the murder himself. But after he thought it through, he decided Chuck wasn't worth blowing up his own life for. Chuck wasn't worth anything at all. John hadn't pressed charges—not for shame. John didn't do shame. He simply didn't want to spend any more time out of his life on Chuck.

The day after the ambush, John had gone to the office like normal. He did everything he usually did, except that he sat down as little as possible. He didn't try to avoid Chuck. He didn't change one damn little thing he did because of Chuck. John was no one's victim. Chuck had done all the avoiding. Chuck kept to himself, maybe rehearsing denials in preparation for John's accusation. John let him squirm in the anxious waiting. Chuck seemed confused and upset that John didn't look wounded, devastated, or cringing in a hole.

And now Bast had murdered Chuck.

John was trying to find the moral high ground. It wasn't happening. The high ground was getting very shaky. And eye for an eye still had a visceral sense of order.

But John was an officer of the law. So was Bast. Bast had really jumped the fence this time. Vigilante justice wasn't justice. That's what his higher consciousness was telling him.

The rest of him said to screw that.

John said, "Thank you."

Bast nodded.

"You read my mind, didn't you?" It was a statement, not a question.

"I did."

"You know all about me," John said. "And you love me anyway."

"What's that tell you, *cher?*"

"That you are seriously fucked."

"*C'est vrai,*" Bast said. It's true.

John said, "Remind me never to piss you off. You take no prisoners."

"I'll be real pissed off if you don't fuck me right now," Bast said.

John closed the space between them in a few long strides and growled into Bast's mouth, the growl of a man in sexual abandon. John seized him and tried to haul him into the bedroom. They didn't make it. Bast stumbled and they both fell on the bare wood floor. John pawed at Bast's clothes and took him there in the doorway.

Bast was taking a shower. John was in Bast's kitchen, making eggs, hash browns, and sausages. When in doubt, do breakfast again. He kept opening and shutting white French Provincial cabinets and drawers, looking for where Bast kept things.

Bast came out of the bedroom, wearing only a dark blue bathrobe that gaped open down to the belt. He leaned in the kitchen doorway, posed in that lazy sexy way of standing Bast had. The robe left a vee-slash view of his hard body. His hair was damp. John had to take the pan of browning onions off the fire and turn off the burner.

Bast was stunning. John looked into his eyes, and his gaze held. He spoke in nearly a whisper, "Are you hungry?"

"I'm starving," Bast said faintly and brushed the overhand knot out of his belt. The front of his robe parted.

John crossed the floor to him, and slid his hands inside Bast's robe. Bast's skin was damp and warm. Bast's eyelashes lowered. His lips were parted, waiting.

Their lips brushed softly. John didn't know how such a simple kiss could have such power to move him. It touched him to the core. John surrounded Bast's body with his arms and drew him in against him. Bast held on tight. They kissed deeply, tongues moving together. Bast lowered his arms and shrugged to let his robe slip off his shoulders, then he tugged at John's tee-shirt. John lifted his arms to let Bast pull his shirt up over his head. He pulled Bast hard against him again and rejoined their kiss. John took a step forward, forcing Bast to step backward toward the bedroom. They lurched together, step by unsteady step, hands groping each other, until Bast ran into the bed and fell back onto the mattress. John stayed upright only long enough to get off his shoes, socks, trousers, and underwear. Bast crab-walked himself all the way onto the bed and welcomed John into his arms and between his legs. John pushed his cock against Bast's cock and hard belly. Bast kept rhythm with his thrusts, gripping and kneading John's buttocks.

John dragged his lips and tongue across Bast's neck and shoulders. Bast murmured, speaking in his native tongue, soft, sensual words of rapture. Bast's voice was like a physical touch. John felt it like the rising heat in his groin. Bast overwhelmed his senses, sound, sight, scent, taste, and touch, touch, touch. Desire welled up, higher and higher, riding sex on sex. Bast's gasp and deep groan, his straining body and the spurts of heated wetness against John's erection sent him soaring into a dazzling climax that went on and on.

John blinked. His eyelashes were wet. He smiled and kissed Bast's face.

Bast's beard shadow was only soft wisps of hair, too fine to scratch. John's own stubble was coarse and prickly, and he'd left a beard burn on Bast's fair neck, but in a few blinks of John's eyes, all the chafing was gone.

John rolled off, onto his back, then drew Bast back in close so Bast's head rested on John's shoulder. John's fingers brushed lightly over Bast's damp skin. He traced Bast's scars with his fingertip, surprised to find that Bast had scars at all—and that he was circumcised. It hadn't occurred to him before to wonder why Bast's foreskin hadn't grown back. "Why doesn't that heal?" John asked, circling the helmet of Bast's cock with his forefinger. Bast forgot the question as soon as John asked it. He moaned.

John let his hand rove elsewhere. "And how come you have scars?" John asked.

Bast found his voice. "I don't know. Anything that happened before I was bitten stayed the way it was."

"But you only have scars as a man. The wolf you doesn't have any."

"I didn't know that. When I'm a wolf I'm doing something other than checking my look."

"Yeah. You're scruffy."

"Am I?"

"Only as a wolf." John caressed Bast's cheek. He said, mystified, "I hated you at first sight and I didn't know why." Technically it had been at second sight in the office. At first sight, under his car, all John could think was *what the fuck?* "I don't know why I hated you. You were the most amazing thing I ever saw."

"That was the shadows talking," Bast said. "They were afraid."

"You knew those were in me?"

"No. I didn't. Not then. Not even when...."

John heard the part Bast couldn't say. *Not even when I found you bare-assed and fucked.*

"I didn't know until the cat saw it in you."

"The—? The black cat?" John remembered it. The cat on the overpass over the Dan Ryan. The cat hissed at them. "*That?* You mean there's something to black cats? I thought that was an old wives' tale."

"Old wives have their shit together. I couldn't read you. I didn't know why, but I guess it was because the shadows were inside. Both of them. You had two shadows in you."

"You said you loved me while I had that shit in there."

"And I didn't have a clue. I saw only you, and you weren't evil. But you were absolutely right about me being not who I said I was. That should have been the tip off. *They* knew what I was. You're a strong man, John. *You* were still in there. I'd have known if the shadows had lodged. You'd be gone, and I can smell a lodged shadow for miles."

"I'd be gone *where?*"

"Wherever it is that people go when they die. I'm not ready to find out exactly where that is."

Die. That was the word John was looking for. "I put a whole clip into you," John said. "Is there any way to kill a loup-garou?"

Immediately, he felt tension in Bast's body. Bast sounded uneasy. "Any reason you want to know, *cher?*"

"Immortality makes no sense." Not that wolf men made any sense to begin with.

"I'm told cremation works. And it's final. If you stake us into the ground with silver, the body decays but the awareness stays for years."

John struggled to form the next question. His words come out quaking. "*How do you know this?*"

"How do you think, *cher?*"

John didn't want to think. He said guardedly, "You know someone this happened to."

"So do you."

Roll Call. 7 Sept 2012. 0800 hours.

First up was Bast, reporting on the Detective Chuck Wallice homicide. "Forensics found no evidence of forced entry—" Bast had to pause for titters and snorts. He let his shoulders slump. "Into the house! Guys, help me here. The victim's house is a fortress. EMS had to break in, and I'm told it was tough to do."

"Then who found him?" Meyers asked.

"EMS received a 911 call at oh four hundred hours from the victim's landline. There was no voice message. The phone was left off the hook. The caller is presumed to be the dom, who was not on the premises when EMS arrived. There were no witnesses, other than the dom. No suspects. Detective Wallice's ex-wife has an alibi. She was visiting her sister."

A murmuring interrupted him, with an exchange of glances. "Chuck was married?" Antwan asked.

"He never mentioned her," Thea said.

"Sure he did," Marv Meyers said. "He was always complaining that a man wasn't allowed to keep his old lady in line anymore."

Bast pushed on. "As for the dom, Forensics has nothing to work with. Neighbors saw no one coming—" Bast lowered his notes and paused again for sniggers. "Will you stop!—or going. There was a half-empty whiskey bottle, open. Two highball glasses, used. One with the decedent's prints. The other participant was wearing gloves, which

I'm told is not unusual with this crowd. There were no lip prints on the second glass. There were no prints on the whip—Guys, I'm trying to give a report here!—Or on the handcuffs, which were left behind, possibly the decedent's personal possessions. The decedent's gear fit him perfectly, which suggests a degree of consent. This suggests an accidental homicide."

The commander said, "You mean Crime Scene found *nothing* on the dom?"

Bast closed his folder. "Commander, the evidence don't even tell what sex the dom was."

After sex, John stood at the railing of Bast's tiny rear deck, and gazed up at the night sky. Bast joined him. Bast's hair was still wet from the shower.

There was a half moon in the sky.

"So you don't dare kill under the full moon," John said.

"Oh, I can kill under the full moon. Manolo was under the full moon."

"Why didn't Manolo become a loup-garou?"

"A shadow can't become loup-garou."

"I mean Manolo, the man."

"Manolo was already dead. Inside the body was only the shadow. I don't dare wound a living man under the full moon."

"Or a woman."

"No, *cher*. There are no female loup-garou."

"Well, they sure turn into something once a month. What's with the throat ripping? Isn't that, literally, overkill?"

"The shadows try to escape out the throat. I close the throat and hold it shut until the body dies. It makes the difference between killing the shadow and setting it free. The shadows are hard to catch in the air."

"You said you closed the throat. You didn't stop at closing it."

Bast nodded. "That was overkill," he confessed.

"Is this only a swamp Catholic thing?"

"When I bite, I'm killing a shadow. I don't ask the shadow if the human being used to be Catholic."

"But the wolf that bit you let *you* live. He obviously didn't tear your throat out."

"I wasn't carrying a shadow. I don't know what made him choose me."

"Did you ask him?"

"No."

"Why don't you?"

That seemed to strike Bast odd. It took him a moment to answer. "I don't even know if he's alive. I don't know where he would be."

"We're detectives. Detect."

They both hit the internet looking for Francois Xavier Duchene. There were a lot of them out there. John included the search terms "wolf" and "loup-garou." He read from one web page. "It says here if you prick a loup-garou with a knife it turns back into a human. Is that true?"

"Or hit me with a car," Bast said. "That works."

"Enough already. You were jaywalking, okay?"

"Found him," Bast said, sounding surprised.

John looked over his shoulder. He was on Facebook. "Frank Duchene. You sure that's the guy?"

Bast pointed at his picture. "That's Francois. He's here in Illinois."

John read his bio. Frank Duchene, PhD, was a Professor of Anthropology at the university. He had a website dedicated to wolf lore.

A search of the university's website told them that the professor had some evening classes, so Bast and John drove out to the university after work the next day. Bast put his Cajun music on the player in the Saab.

John watched the passing cityscape out the car window, trying hard to keep his hands off Bast while he was at the wheel. "I just can't see you pulling catfish out of logs, René."

"Only when I was a boy," Bast said. "It was good in the Bayou. Then I was bit. When folks noticed I wasn't getting older, I had to leave. Folks thought it was Voodoo."

"Is there anything to Voodoo?"

"Only if you believe in the latent powers of dead chickens."

"I don't know what I believe anymore."

"When I came to the city I carried a Derringer. I was a cop. New Orleans was worse than the Wild West in those days. I didn't know how evil evil could be. I was buried there. And we don't bury people on the Bayou."

Evening sunlight limned Bast's cheek with gold. "You don't feel da fear so much when you don't have a beating heart or a breath or a clawing stomach. Bones. Bones just abide."

Bast had said Krieg buried him. John never let himself believe that Bast might be speaking literally. "Krieg," John said.

Bast nodded once. "The shadow inhabits Krieg now. The shadow's host was Le Carpentier in those days and he was a slave auctioneer. He bought and sold people. He had me clubbed, den he drove a silver spike into my chest and buried me alive in da levee."

John knew Bast had been bitten in the 1860s. He'd assumed that Krieg buried him shortly before Katrina. Now Bast was talking about a slave auctioneer....

Bast had been buried alive sometime during the fucking Civil War.

"Jesus, Mary, and Joe."

"The flesh died. I rotted. I...abided. Then I—I don't know what. I thought I was dying. I'm not sure what happen." His accent was getting thick again. "I think it was Katrina. When da levee wash away, it had to be then something happen. I don't know. I'm not sure how I become a wolf again. As long as I was aware, I was alive. If let myself slip away, I knew that was death. Then I couldn't hang on. I thought I was dying. It must have been sleep I think. I had dreams of being carried. And my mother teaching me to hunt. I don't remember being a human child again. First thing I knew I was loup-garou, licking a woman's leg. And when I changed into a man I was this." He looked at his own hands on the steering wheel as if he found them odd. They were long-fingered, masculine but finer than John's. "And it was 2007."

"I am falling down a rabbit hole," John said.

"I had a first edition of *Alice's Adventures in Wonderland*," Bast said from somewhere in left field.

"How did you *live?*"

"You need to realize, I didn't have a brain. No temporal lobe—that part of the brain that says are we there yet? After you get past that first part when you want to die, time don't exist. You're not thinking. You're just aware. No heart to pound. No nerves to fray. No gut to twist. But you can lose your grip and fade out. Oblivion is right *there*. It would've been so easy to just...go."

"You have a strong will, René."

Bast shook his head, with a conspiratorial wrinkle to his nose. "Coward," he offered instead. "I'm afraid to meet my maker. And I don't mean this *bougre* we're going to see."

Chapter Ten

Dr. Frank Duchene was a fiftyish, lanky academic with freckles and reddish grayish hair. He looked up over his wire-rimmed glasses as John and Bast entered his office without knocking.

Bast flashed his star. "René Bast. Chicago PD."

Duchene wasn't exactly afraid, but he did have the look of a man considering whether to jump out the window or face the fire.

Dr. Duchene said something that sounded like *fee d' puTAN*. It didn't sound like a compliment, but Bast said, "Well, as a matter fact, yes."

John guessed Duchene had called Bast a son of a bitch.

The professor looked hard at Bast through his wire-rims, and said, not quite sure, "*Sebastien?*"

"My name is Bast these days."

Duchene turned gray eyes to John and asked, "And what do *you* call him?"

John knew what word Duchene was looking for. John said, "Hell, I'd still call him that if his name was Fred."

"Why are you here, 'Detective Bast?'" Duchene pronounced his title with heavy irony.

Bast stood with his weight way back on one leg, his long body in a sinuous curve. He regarded Duchene out of the tops of his eyes. "I came for information, but now that I see you I just want to beat the shit out of you."

Duchene's eyes shifted to John, waiting for the answer to the same question from him.

John glanced to Bast and back to Duchene. "Oh, me.

I'm just here for the information. I don't want any shit."

"Are you garou?" Duchene asked John.

"No. I'm Batman."

Duchene looked up at Bast. "I didn't have a choice, Sebastien. You know we don't."

Choice. That probably meant the life-changing bite Duchene had given Bast.

Bast opened his hands, presenting himself. "Then whose idea was it to make me—this?"

Duchene dropped his gaze. "It wasn't mine, Sebastien. I haven't a clue what made me do that. I just...did it. If there was anyone's mind behind it, I don't know. It took you long enough to ask."

"Did it really?" Bast said, soft venom in his voice. "I hardly noticed the time."

Bast was glaring at Duchene with a look like loathing. John followed Bast's gaze, zeroed menacingly in on Duchene's throat. John was afraid Bast was about to tear Duchene's throat out. Then John noticed that the professor was wearing a little silver cross around his neck. Bast demanded, "What's that about?"

It took Duchene a moment to realize what Bast was referring to. "Oh." He lifted a freckled hand to the cross at his throat. "It's tin," Duchene said. "Protective camouflage."

Loup-garou couldn't touch silver.

It was Duchene's turn to ask a question. "Where have you been, Sebastien?"

"I kind of went underground for a while," Bast said. "Tell me about us. The loup-garou."

Duchene's gray eyebrows gave a brief lift. "You want to narrow that question down a little bit, *frère*?"

"How does a loup-garou come back to life?"

Duchene sat back in his chair, relaxing, apparently realizing he wasn't about to get the shit beaten out of him. He looked very professorial in his Oxford shirt and gray vest. "That depends on how the death occurred."

"Okay, here's a scenario. Suppose a loup-garou gets staked with silver—"

"Then if someone pulls the silver out, he will revive," Duchene finished for him.

"No, take it further. The loup-garou gets staked, buried with the silver stake, and rots away. Can he come back?"

"If he hasn't given up, the bones can endure. Then a real she-wolf can revive the garou. And she *will*, if she comes near living bones. She is compelled to. It's a drive as powerful as sex. If the animus is still in the bones, she will take the living bones into her body."

"Eat them," John said, revolted.

Duchene gave an unjudgmental shrug. "The animus seeks to be reborn. The she-wolf takes in the essence of the garou and reincarnates him."

"How?" Bast's question came out a bark.

"When the she-wolf consumes the bones, she conceives. The next born pup of the she-wolf will be a single birth, male. The dam is a dumb animal. The wolf pup is an animal while he is a pup. When the pup is full grown, he has an impulse to approach human beings. At a touch of human blood, the wolf's human awareness returns. He becomes what he was before, a garou, a manwolf. The animus is the essential being. The body is only the house. The body is immortal so long as the immortal animus is in it. The body dies when the animus leaves. Don't ask me where it goes. I don't know. Buried alive, the garou can survive without food or water. The flesh can decay, but the bones live as long as the animus stays and keeps the will to live. I've heard of garou living as long as ten years in the ground."

"That long?" Bast said faintly.

"*C'est vrai*," Duchene assured him. "It's unimaginable."

John found the mirror on Duchene's office wall. It was smaller than Bast's. "I got one for you, professor. What are shadows?"

"Evil!" Duchene answered without pause. "Pure evil! They act like viruses. A shadow takes over the core of its prey. It inserts its own essence into the human shell and becomes the being's whole existence. The humanity is gone. The evil remains until it wants to leave. As soon as it's gone, the host shell dies. The cause of death is usually diagnosed as heart failure. The shadow doesn't need a body to survive."

Bast walked to Duchene's window, lifted his hands to either jamb, and gazed out. "Do you remember Le Carpentier?"

"I do," Duchene answered to Bast's turned back. "The shadow inside him most recently took over the body of a man named Krieg, grandson of an SS officer who escaped to Uruguay after the war. He's in Chicago now."

"I know him," Bast said to the window.

"Then you can answer something for me." Duchene dove into a stack of papers at one end of his desk and brought out a rust-foxed sheet of paper that may have been white once upon a time. "Krieg was bequeathed a walled section of a cemetery in the old part of Chicago. The sanctuary was willed to Krieg by his shadow's previous incarnation, an organized crime boss named Camastra back in the 1940s. This is Camastra's document. It's a map of the graves within the sanctuary. The walled sanctuary dates back to 1810, and the family name isn't any one of the shadow's previous incarnations. The family name of the plot is Argent."

Bast flinched and turned around to stare at Duchene.

John took one step backward. "Should I be ducking and hiding behind a major appliance?"

"No," Bast said, his voice dead calm. "But we might consider it." He meant himself and Duchene.

Duchene spoke aside to John, "Argent means Silver. There is no family by the name of Argent who ever owned that section of the graveyard."

Bast strode to the desk, and snatched the map out of Duchene's hand. "Is it in driving distance?"

As Bast drove his Saab out to the cemetery, John turned around to look at Dr. Duchene in the back seat. "So, Yoda, why do you guys change into wolves? I mean, why is it wolves? Why not owls or pussycats?"

Duchene actually had an answer for that. "*Canis* decided a long time ago to throw his lot in with humankind. Ever since the first wolf came to a caveman's fire, his duty has been to protect and serve. Some wolves became dogs. Some wolves became garou to hunt down shadows."

"But there are still real wolves, aren't there?"

"Of course."

"So what's the deal between dogs and cats?"

John thought he was being flip, but Dr. Duchene had an answer for that too. "Saber-tooth cats used to hunt man. *Canis* remembers."

That was a long time to hold a grudge. "How far back do shadows go?"

"Evil has been with us always. I know that Hitler and Idi Amin were shadow carriers."

"No shit?"

"Those shadows are particularly malignant. They survived the deaths of their carriers. I don't know who they're in now. I like to imagine that one died inside Osama Bin Laden, but I wouldn't count on it."

Bast drove in through the cemetery gates and past the steepled Catholic church.

Duchene pointed a bony forefinger up at a light pole. "Security cameras."

"Dummies," John said.

Bast nodded.

"Dummies?" Duchene asked.

"Low cost vandal deterrent," John said.

"Then we're not being photographed?"

"No," John said. "Why? Are we going to be vandalizing something?"

"We might," Bast said. He parked the car.

The cemetery was very old. The oldest sections were scantly tended, the edges gone entirely to weeds and scrub trees. The old quarry stone grave markers here were weathered and unreadable. You could just make out the vague shape of a dove here, a cross there.

In one of the most neglected areas stood an enclosure, its tall walls built of great limestone blocks. Its door, so badly tarnished that it was purple-black, was embossed with the name ARGENT. Bast reached for the ring to open it, then snatched his hand back, and took several steps away. Duchene was standing halfway to the parking lot. Bast said softly, "John, you're gonna have to open this for us."

John stepped forward. The doors were silver plate, if not solid silver. And they were bolted from the inside.

Bast and Duchene were conferring on how to jimmy the lock. John took a running start, leapt for the top edge of the stone wall, and hoisted himself up and over. He lifted the crossbar and opened the doors from the inside.

Bast entered, his head down like a spooked dog, the hair on his forearms standing up.

Duchene crept in. He moved his palm close to the stone walls, like he might over a stove burner to see if it was on. "There's silver in the mortar."

"Argent doesn't want you two getting in here," John said.

"I don't want to be here," Duchene said.

The plots were laid out in an eight by eight square. Most of them were unused or unmarked. John counted only six headstones. There were no names engraved on the stones, only dates, and even then it was only one date. The dates ranged between 1810 and 1915.

Duchene withdrew Camastra's brittle map from its protective folder and read off names as he pointed at individual stones. "Matthew Argent. Luke Argent. Mark Argent. John Argent. Peter Argent. Paul Argent."

"Very Biblical these Argents," Bast said.

"They're all guys," John said, fresh in his mind that there were no female loup-garou.

"It's not a family name," Duchene said in quiet horror. "These are not dearly beloved in this ground."

The motion caught John's eye—falling clothes. A pepper-black wolf was pacing back and forth amid the gravestones, sniffing the earth, its hackles up.

John stood with Duchene, watching Bast the wolf pace. "I notice you keep saying garou, Yoda. Not loup-garou. Why?"

"I don't know why anyone says loup-garou," Duchene said. "Loup-garou literally means wolf-manwolf. I feel ridiculous saying it. Garou is enough."

John called to the wolf. "Bast! Give it up. You're not going to smell anything six feet under. We need to come back here with ground-penetrating radar."

Bast, a man again, pulled on his clothes. John looked away. His cock was stirring and this wasn't the place for lust. He told Duchene, "We have a GPR in the police department."

Bast, behind him, added, "But it's only good for a few

feet down, not a full six feet. When the police are looking for a hidden grave, it's usually a shallow one."

The police department's GPR was a hand-held thing that looked like something a beachcomber would use to look for lost jewelry after all the tourists had gone.

Dr. Duchene smiled. "The anthro department includes archaeology. We have much more muscular equipment than that."

The next weekend, John and Bast came back to the cemetery, where they met Dr. Duchene in his pickup truck, towing a trailer bearing the anthropology department's ground-penetrating radar. The machine looked like a bulked-up lawnmower with a computer screen on it.

Duchene rolled the machine over the graves inside Argent's sanctuary. He needed to do a lot of adjusting of the instruments.

"Something wrong with your equipment?" Bast asked.

"No. Not the GPR. The graves," Duchene said, a nervous note in his scratchy voice. "They're eight foot deep."

John didn't want to sound ignorant in front of the professor. He muttered aside to Bast, "So?"

Bast gave an eyebrow shrug. "Don't look at me. We don't bury folks in the Bayou."

"They're too deep. Something's wrong." Duchene sounded alarmed. "No one buries the dead that deep unless they're making sure something doesn't come back up."

"Like plague?" John asked.

"Usually. But not this time. There's not much plague in Chicago, and not over a span of a hundred years," Duchene said. "And no one leaves grave gifts with plague victims."

"Grave gifts?"

"There are objects in the graves," Duchene said. Gravely.

Bast stalked over to see the machine's readout for himself. "What objects?"

"Metal crosses. Spikes. They're not around the body. They're *in* the body."

Bast got impatient. "Answer the real question, Francois. Are the objects silver?"

"I can't tell from this. But I would bet my weight in silver that they are. The silver in the mortar in these walls isn't to keep garou from getting in. *Argent doesn't want garou getting out.*"

"Those are wolf men down there," John said.

Even though cremation was more final, John supposed it was hard to burn a body, and this was more cruel. That's why you need the wall. When you bury people alive you want some privacy.

Bast was looking at the screen of the GPR. He said in sudden panic, "We've got to get them out. Now. *Now.*"

John came over to the machine to see what Bast had seen. The images were fuzzy, but clearly the bones were lying in contorted positions of perfect agony.

Duchene sounded tired. "Sebastien, it's pointless. These graves are at least a hundred years old."

"They could still be alive!"

Duchene's face went slack, daunted. It seemed he recognized the voice of someone who knew exactly how long a garou could endure underground. He argued as if it pained him. "We can't go digging up graves. I can't even excuse that as archaeology. And there's no way to tell from GPR images if the bones are still *viable* or, more likely, they gave up many, many years ago."

"But you know a way to tell," John said.

Chasing Shadows

John and Bast met Duchene back at the graveyard on Sunday evening.

Duchene had got himself a she-wolf from a rescue organization. She'd been someone's exotic pet before her family realized what they'd gotten into. She was young, mostly white, the only color on her a sandy patch on her back in the shape of a saddle and a black diamond on her tail. She had a small lupine mane and a grandma-eating smile.

Set free from Duchene's pickup truck, she trotted immediately to John, her head down, her tongue hanging out. John reached to pet her head.

"Watch it," Duchene warned. "She's head-shy and she hates to have her ears touched."

Too late. John was ruffling her fur and playing with her ears.

"Or not."

Duchene had also brought an auger to bore a narrow hole deep enough to let the she-wolf catch the smell of the bones.

Bast's breaths were deep and fast as the auger drilled into the earth of the most recent grave, the one marked 1915. "If we find life, we're going to be tearing up a grave. How do we explain that?"

"You'll need to get a warrant on some grounds—" Duchene started.

"No!" Bast shouted, staring wildly at Duchene. "You don't get it. I mean *we*." He motioned between himself and the she-wolf. "*We* will be tearing up the grave. Even if you think you can stop her, you won't be stopping me, *frère*."

Duchene bristled. "This is *your* dig, *frère*. You explain it."

John lifted his hands, signaling for calm. "No warrant," he said quietly. "The shadows built this wall for privacy. It worked for them, it can work for us. The only question is are we going need more she-wolves?"

Bast said, "We can only hope."

The auger reached a depth of eight feet. Duchene hauled it out of the earth, and John led the she-wolf over to have a sniff. She nosed the fresh earth around the hole, acting like any dog in any park in the world.

John touched Bast's arm. "I'm sorry."

Duchene set the auger to drilling the next most recent grave. Peter Argent from 1900. Bast trickled earth back into the first drill hole. He murmured, "*Requiescat in pacem*," and crossed himself.

The third and fourth drill holes left them nothing but dirty and tired. The she-wolf hadn't reacted to any of the graves so far. The fifth, Luke Argent, didn't interest her either.

"They're all dead," Duchene lamented. He wiped his dirty hand across his eyes, giving him the look of a freckled raccoon.

They were all the way back to 1810 now—to Matthew Argent—the oldest grave.

By now it was too dark to see. They were working by the tiny LED light on John's key ring. Anything brighter might attract attention to the sanctuary.

Duchene had lost heart. "It doesn't seem possible he could be alive." He looked to Bast for surrender. 1810 was over twice as long as Bast had lasted in the ground.

Bast smoldered.

It was hopeless. But Bast needed to know. John decided it. "We're here."

Duchene positioned the auger over Matthew Argent's grave.

At a depth of six feet, Duchene brought the auger up to clean off the screw. "I hate to say I told you so. And I truly hate to now, b—" The dirt began to fly. John ducked, flinging his arms over his head. He spat flying motes off his lips.

The she-wolf was digging, in a frenzy. Bast's clothes were suddenly on the ground, and the pepper-black wolf was digging with her.

John got out of the way of the flying clods. Dr. Duchene looked toward John, as if for permission.

John shrugged and lifted his hand. "Hey. Go for it, Yoda."

"Hold my glasses." Duchene handed his wire-rims to John. Then a wiry red wolf was in there, triple arcs of earth flying.

John watched the stars slowly turn. They had to get this done before daylight.

The wolves were getting down deep into it. The earth was packed tighter, harder to dig, and the she-wolf was getting territorial, snapping at Bast and Duchene.

Then John heard a savage growl. He looked down. The she-wolf had her nose wrinkled back up her face, and her lip rippled ferociously at Bast and Duchene.

The red wolf leapt out of the hole, tail between its legs. Bast climbed out as a man. "John, see if you can deal with your girlfriend."

John looked down with his LED. "You've struck bone."

The white wolf was chewing on a fibula. She looked up sharply as if about to snap, then saw it was John, and let him climb down with her. She let John pack her a to-go bucket. It was an old grave, so it didn't smell bad. This had been a surreal year for John so far, so collecting bones in an eight-foot deep grave didn't seem quite as bizarre as it might have once upon a time.

Duchene sent down a rope for John to tie onto the bucket handle as he would on an archaeological excavation.

John climbed out of the grave and started hauling up the bucket. He called to the wolf. "Come on, Madonna. Let's go. Bring your bone."

"Madonna?" Bast looked to Duchene. "You named her Madonna?"

"*I* didn't name her anything," Duchene said. They both looked to John.

"This is gonna be a virgin birth isn't it?" John said.

The white wolf sprang out of the hole, the fibula between her jaws. She lay down by the bucket, and gnawed, as Bast and Duchene, in wolf form again, back-filled the grave.

They made their way back to Duchene's truck and Bast's Saab as the sky was beginning to show a gray haze at the eastern horizon. Duchene had brought a load of flowers in the bed of his truck, just in case someone caught them in the graveyard with dirty hands.

Then the wolf refused get into the truck, and she wouldn't let Duchene touch the bucket of bones.

Bast turned to John. "Does your apartment allow pets?"

"*I* don't allow human remains in my apartment," John said. "We're going home with you tonight. This morning. Whatever the hell time it is."

John picked up the bucket, and loaded the wolf and the bucket into the back seat of Bast's Saab.

Duchene climbed into his pickup and let his shoulders slump, sorrowful, as if he'd attended a funeral instead of a resurrection. "Hell of a dig. And I can't publish it."

John rode in the back seat of Bast's car, brooding. The wolf had fallen asleep with her head on John's thigh. Bast was a comforting presence at the wheel. John felt a sweet ache for him, like warmth after a long bitter cold. His thoughts wandered. The world as he knew it had turned upside down and he tried to rearrange the pieces.

John spoke, insistent, "Lori wasn't a bad person."

"I never said she was," Bast said at the wheel.

"Why did the shadow pick her? She wasn't a Krieg."

"Shadows go where they can cause despair."

"I should've done more to help her. She was sick. She needed me."

"She wasn't sick. She was *gone*. There was no way you were going to win that one."

"I could've. I know I could've, if I'd known what was happening. Lori said she was possessed. She was still Lori then. I should've believed her."

"You're a rescuer, John."

"It's in the job description."

"No. *You* are. You live for that. That's why you're chasing down criminals instead of bulking up with illegal substances and playing shortstop for big money."

"Well. Yeah."

"And you have a hard time asking for help. In fact, you don't do it."

Bast and John barely had time to wash off the dirt and find clean clothes before they had to report to work.

On coming home again, Bast found the white wolf, Madonna, had been too occupied with her bones to trash his place. And she turned out to be housebroken. John let her out the back door to the yard. Bast wearily took off his sport jacket and shrugged out of his holster. He let them drop to the floor. He was dead tired, but not too tired for sex.

Neither, it seemed, was John. He'd already got rid of his jacket and tie in the car. As soon as the screen door fell shut, John was stalking back across the floor, heavy lidded and scowling with lust, unbuttoning his shirt as he came.

Stock still and breathless, Bast waited on John's forceful advance. Time slowed down, dreamlike. John closed the distance between them and pulled Bast's shirt from the confines of his trousers. John's warm, callused palms slid up Bast's back and pulled him in tight. John's bare chest with its scattered bristle of coarse hair crushed against Bast's own chest. John kissed his mouth roughly. Bast's tongue welcomed his hunger. John's clothed erection ground against his own. Bast gripped John's hard, hard ass.

In a moment, they tore apart.

Bast got out of his trousers and his thong, almost falling over in his haste. John pushed his own trousers down and kicked them off. He seized Bast's hand and led him into the bedroom. He threw himself onto Bast's bed, pulling Bast down on top of him.

Bast moved with him, riding, naked cock to naked cock. John's hands held his ass, urging him on. John's mouth was hot against Bast's shoulder. Bast felt the grazing of his teeth against his skin. Something inside Bast's groin turned, melting.

Hot wet jets spurted against Bast's cock. Bast caught in his breath in a moment of sheer wonder. His balls grew taut. Every muscle strained. Climax gripped hard and released in throbbing waves against his lover's sex. Bast shut his eyes and gasped. Pinpricks of sweat tingled on his skin. He shivered. Then, at last, he exhaled a groaning sigh of bliss.

John immediately fell asleep, holding Bast in his arms.

Bast stayed awake. He gazed at John's peaceful face. John's beard stubble looked gold in the evening sunlight that streamed through the open window. Bast nuzzled John's bristly chin and inhaled his scent. The smell was musky, erotic, and masculine. Bast wanted to hold this moment forever. He wanted John to stay with him this way, always. Bast knew he could make that happen at the full moon. But it was too much to ask. *That* needed to be offered.

And we have time.

In the following days, John moved more things to Bast's house. Bast was checking his notebook computer. John kissed him on the back of his neck. "What you got?"

Bast said, "An e-mail from Francois."

"Who?"

"Frank Duchene."

"Oh yeah. Yoda," John said. Bast hadn't turned and kissed him back. "Bad news?"

Bast hesitated, as if he couldn't answer the question. "He says there's a new grave in the Argent family plot."

Chapter Eleven

John felt a prickling on the back of his neck.

Bast e-mailed Duchene back with questions, but he got an out-of-office reply. Dr. Duchene was out with a class archaeological expedition. He would be back at the end of the month.

Bast and John drove out to the cemetery without him. They waited until the parking lot was empty to get out of the car.

They hiked out under the blind cameras to the untidy back of the graveyard. "This feels wrong," John said.

"I'd be surprised if it felt right," Bast said.

The door to the Argent sanctuary faced the rear of the cemetery, so Bast and John approached from the blind side.

Bast and John circled wide to the far side of the enclosure. The sanctuary's silver doors stood gaping open. Bast and John could see inside, an open pit, a new gravestone. They didn't move close enough to read it, but to guess from the length of the engraving the headstone might have read *Sebastien Argent*.

John saw the hair at the back of Bast's head lift.

"*Nous sommes foutu.*"

Too late, John's old geometry class came back to him. He and Bast were standing in a straight line from the headstone through the parted doors. Someone had deliberately maneuvered them to stand precisely on this trajectory. Too late because already John heard the hiss of sizzling air from the weed-choked trees straight behind them. A dull thunk sounded immediately at his side. Bast was falling to his knees. John sank down with him, holding him. A silver bolt protruded though Bast's midsection. Blood bubbled from his lips.

Bast bent over. The end of the silver shaft stuck out his back. Bast's breaths gurgled. "Dey get out drough de droat."

They get out through the throat.

John looked back. A grinning, vast, silver-blue man stepped out from the undergrowth—Krieg with a crossbow. His neck was covered in silver chains. He swaggered, gloating over Bast, who lay agonized and twisting in John's arms, helpless.

John drew his Glock. Krieg's teeth appeared as a white gash within his dark silver face. "Go ahead. Murder me, little policeman. My next incarnation will visit you in Tamms." The maximum security prison was one of the worst. Violent criminals went to Tamms since Illinois couldn't execute murderers anymore. A cop killing a civilian with his service weapon might expect to land there. "You'll know me by my laugh."

Krieg spat on Bast. Bast reacted as if burned by acid.

Bast couldn't bear the touch of silver.

I can.

All in one motion, John stood up, yanking the silver bolt out of Bast body. Bast's muscles clung to it tight, dragging at it, but John was in the grip of an adrenaline rage. It gave him strength beyond his own considerable power. He pulled the long bolt free and thrust its shaft through Krieg's silver necklaces, and he twisted and twisted and twisted—hard and fast, like steering the wheel of a ship in a storm. He fell as Krieg fell, landing atop the bucking, kicking mass, but John didn't let go. Blows from Krieg's hammy hands buffeted his head. John felt the pop of the windpipe giving way under his winch, then felt the esophagus collapsing. *They get out through the throat.* John needed to lock the shadow things inside Krieg until Krieg was dead in order to kill the shadows. The big man's mindless thrashing weakened, but it wasn't over. John hauled the bolt around another turn. John glanced over to Bast, who was in agony. John planted one foot flat on the ground to get up and go to him, but Bast flapped him away with a strengthless hand. "Keep—keep—"

"Keep at it?" John guessed, still holding the bolt. He tried to twist it even tighter. His muscles seared like live electrical wires.

Bast gasped, "Don't. Let. Go. *Fin*. Finish."

"Damn it, Bast—"

"Finish!"

John thought the thing might be dead. Still he strained to keep the noose tight around the thick neck. He shut his eyes and screwed up his face, hanging on until he couldn't.

Strangled with pain, Bast choked, his voice bubbling, "*C'est fini.*"

John let go and scrambled to Bast, dragging his hands on the grass to get some of the blood off. He rolled Bast face up. Bast pawed at his own bleeding midriff. "Get it out. Get it out." John searched frantically for a second silver bolt. There was no other bolt. All the blood was from one wound. "I already got it. René, I got it." Bast was still begging, "Get it out. Get it out." His hands fluttered around the wound.

"It's out! I choked Krieg with it!"

Bast writhed. "Get it out." His face screwed up in a tortured grimace.

The wound wasn't healing the way Bast's bullet wounds had quickly closed over in the park. It was still bleeding. Bast was pale as death.

A piece of silver must've broken off from the bolt. That was all John could think. It was still in there, inside the wound.

John didn't even try to warn Bast this was going to hurt like hell—the pain was already past that. John thrust two fingers into the narrow wound. *Don't be gentle, just get it.* He felt around, Bast's sinews fighting him. Bast screamed with his mouth shut. John broke into a fiery sweat. He thought he felt the edge of a hard chip against his forefinger, then lost it. He mumbled strings of curses, fishing. Found it.

John got the hard chip between his slippery forefinger and middle finger and pulled it out. It was silver.

Bast's wound closed up after his retreating fingers. Bast lay panting in relief, his mouth open, gulping the air. He was literally drained.

"How do I report this?" John lifted one bloody hand at the scene and let it drop. "This is the end of my career."

"It's the end of more than your career," Bast said between gasps. "John, this is life without parole. I know you want to be straight up about this, but there's no legal excuse for garroting a man. And that's not what you did anyway. You didn't kill a man. You trapped an ancient evil inside a soulless bag. But that don't look so good on a police report." He was talking sloppy. He was severely shaken.

"No," John agreed. *The truth will set you free of your badge.*

"You not gonna report this," Bast said, his breaths coming longer.

"Yoda set us up," John said.

"Francois is loup-garou," Bast said to the treetops. "He can't. It should've tipped me off when his out-of-office reply was on a dot com e-mail address instead of a dot edu address. I missed that. I'm not used to this millennium."

He lifted himself up on his elbows, quivering all over, dehydrated. His hair was wet with sweat and tears. He sniffed. "So. What I gonna done did is tamper with this crime scene. Take a walk."

"Give me your clothes," John said. "There's a stream down there."

Bast stripped and left his clothes in a small pile in the scrubby grass.

John tramped down to the creek, trying to keep on the stones, disturbing as little of the weeds and trees as he could, and he rinsed their clothes and their shoes in the cold running water.

He dragged his wet things back on, and carried Bast's clothes back up to the sanctuary and parked them in the grass. John heard Bast moving inside the enclosure, doing something. John said, "You're stuff's here."

Bast called out, "Wait in the car."

Bast returned to the parking lot in a little over an hour, wearing his damp clothes. They clung to his lean frame, outlining the muscles in his healed midriff.

He didn't look as thin as he had after John shot him. John asked, "Are you hungry?"

"I ate," Bast said.

"Squirrel?"

Bast shook his head. "Groundhog. Crawfish."

Roll Call. 29 Sept 2012. 0800 Hours.

The commander announced, "Our friend Krieg was found dead in St. James Cemetery, buried in a shallow grave in a plot he owns, an apparent hit by the Knights

Templar. The Templars are silent. FBI's not sure it wasn't an inside job by Krieg's own organization. This is just FYI. This is not our case. We can put Krieg to bed."

The detectives applauded.

John spent the rest of the work day jumping out of his skin. Finally alone with Bast in his car, John hissed at him, "*You framed the Templars?*"

Bast looked really too pleased with himself, his eyes forming merry crescents. He gave a wolfish smile. "The Templars didn't deny it. They want credit. It makes them look terrifying."

"I don't understand what was Krieg doing out without his bodyguards. He was taking a big risk there." A monumental risk as it turned out.

"No risk. You keep thinking Krieg had an existence separate from the shadow. The shadow was done with Krieg's body. The shadow just wanted to bury me before it moved into a new house."

Bast took John to his apartment. He walked him to the front door. John turned on the step. "Come up?"

Bast stayed where he was, gazing up at him, mouth open, as if searching for words. He blurted, "John, I want you to move in with me. Madonna wants you there."

John took a step down. He put his arms loosely around Bast's waist and brushed his lips against his. "Madonna does, hmm?"

A motion made him look left.

A black SUV with dark windows approached from nine o'clock, too fast. John couldn't see the plate for the headlight glare. "I don't like the look of this—" *Crack!* John was crumpling, *Crack!* Blood flowing between his fingers holding his belly.

Bast was on his cell, calling the codes, his other hand trying to staunch the bleeding.

***

John woke up in ICU, oxygen tubes at his nose. Nice stuff, oxygen. There were more tubes connected to machines he didn't know what did. There were lots of transparent tubes with blood in them. He learned that he'd taken two hollow points. It wasn't like the first time he'd been shot. That had been an armor-piercing round. That shot had gone straight through, not stopping to piss on anything.

Hollow points entered a body, mushroomed out, and stayed to trash the place. They'd done critical damage to several vital organs.

"Should I be shopping for new ones?" John asked the nurse.

"We're shopping. We'll get you spare parts, Detective."

"How many people are in front of me? On the organ list. Lists."

"You have priority."

"That means I'm hosed," John said. The worst off went to the head of the class.

An officer from Patrol stopped in to question John. "Why did Gustav Brugge shoot you?"

"I don't know who shot me. I don't know that name."

The officer showed him a picture. John recognized him. It was Krieg's majordomo. "I saw this man once. He works for Krieg. I don't know his name. Why does he look dead in this picture?"

At last Bast was allowed into John's room. The sight shocked Bast, even though Bast knew what to expect. John gave a weak near-smile. Bast leaned down and kissed him on the lips. "Are you in pain?"

"Nope." John looked at all of his tubes. "One of these is a real nice controlled substance. How are you doing?"

"Crazy out of my mind. Otherwise, all right."

"Patrol was in here, asking questions. I didn't see anything."

"They grilled me too. I got the shooter's plate number and the make and model of the SUV. Patrol found it. Krieg's majordomo was dead at the wheel. An apparent heart attack, they say."

"He had a shadow in him," John guessed.

"Yeah. And that shadow is in the wind now. I'm sorry, John. It should have been me."

"Screw that. Are we in trouble? With the Department?"

"Other than being at death's door, you're not in trouble."

"Are you?"

"Not with the Department."

"Can you stay with me?"

"Yeah."

They talked for a while, nothing of importance, except how was Madonna. They talked circles around the ostrich in the room. Bast broke first. He said, "The moon is full."

John rolled his head on the pillow toward the window. "Can't see it."

John knew what Bast was really telling him. Bast waited at the bedside. It was John's decision to make.

It was John's choice. John had to already know the choice was there. And still he was silent.

That was his choice.

No. Bast couldn't let this pass without saying something. "John, there's something you're not asking me."

John turned the statement back on him. "There's something *you're* not asking *me*."

The moon was full.

Bast hung his head. John was *not* asking Bast to make him a loup-garou, and Bast wasn't asking John if he wanted to be immortal like Bast. "The thing is," Bast said with difficulty, "If I bite you, you also get the fur coat and the job with it. Shadow Hunter. That part's not a choice. You do it because you can't not do it. Do you want to be chasing shadows for the rest of your very very very long life?"

"No," John said. "The thing is, do you want me to live?"

"More than anything. Is that the only thing you're not sure about? Because I'll bite you right now. But do you really want to live this way? Or."

John nodded that he understood.

Bast saw his mind churning. Bast knew what it meant.

Or do you want to go to your God and see your son again.

John said, "I needed to know if living was an option."

"It's more than an option. I need you, John. I'm begging."

"I need to think."

Bast was surprised, stung, and panicked.

John didn't need telling not to wait too long. But then, waiting too long was itself a decision.

John needed to think. That told Bast something. And Bast didn't like what it told him. Bast felt ill with panic.

Bast could make the decision for John. And Bast badly wanted to do it. Still, it was John's life. Bast whispered, "Please stay with me."

John took his hand, squeezed it with surprising strength. "We're not there yet."

He rested a few moments. Then he said, his eyes shut, "So many things I wanted to do with my little guy. I never got to coach his little league team. Teach him how to drive. Give the sex talk. I got no idea how I was gonna do that. Wish I had the chance."

He was talking like the decision was already made.

"You're not afraid of dying," Bast said dully.

"No. Not in a hurry either. Just not...not holding on too tight."

Bast said faintly, "You're just biding time until you see your boy again."

"You saw that in me, huh? That's all I was doing before I met you."

Bast squeezed his knee. "Hold on tighter."

Bast stayed in a chair, his head resting on the bed. No one made him leave. Hospitals had changed since the bad old days. They figured out that what helped heal people was the company of loved ones.

Either that or they knew John was done for and didn't want him to be alone at the end.

Bast looked out the window. The full moon getting lower in the sky.

He closed his eyes for a moment.

He woke with a start and looked toward the window in a cold panic. The moon was setting.

It was too late.

The decision was irrevocably made now. He felt a stunned, hollow disbelief. *This is it.* The end of everything. Bast existed in a weird shell of lonely. He laid his head on the pillow with John's. Bast breathed him in, felt his scant heat, drank in the last moments of their lives. John was still here. Bast determined to cling to every last moment. John was still here until the moment when he was not.

The end was written now. *We'll die together then.* Bast had been touched once in love. *I have lived. Now I can die.* Bast would stay with John through the sacred passage.

And then follow him.

He softly gave John a kiss that could be goodbye. He held on to that moment to make it last forever.

Chapter Twelve

John was awake, touching Bast's hair. "René."
Bast lifted his head. His face felt tight with tear-salt. "Yeah, *cher*."
Somewhere a siren wailed, coming closer.
John rolled his head on the pillow, nodded toward the window. Ambulance lights flashed red against the window pane.
"It's just a siren," Bast said. That could be anything. This emergency didn't have to be an organ donor.
"I know what it is," John said. "Danny told me."
"I don't believe in voices from beyond," Bast said.
"*You* don't, huh?"
But suddenly there were people moving fast in the hall, and a nurse in the room doing something with John's tubing. She winked at him.
"Showtime, John."

John opened his eyes. He was still in the curtained space where they'd prepped him for surgery. But Bast was here now.
"Hi," John said—tried to. His mouth was dry.
"Do you remember me coming in?"
"When?"
"An hour ago."
"No."
"It was like talking to a dormouse and a March hare."

"When are they going to operate?"

"They already did."

"Oh," John said. "Any chance I can get a drink of water?"

John was moved into another hospital room. The dialysis machine was gone. The words "flying colors" had been used.

Bast stood in one corner, his arms so tightly crossed he was hugging himself. He was scowling.

John said, "You don't look like a man whose lover just beat the Reaper."

Bast seemed disgruntled. No, Bast seemed pissed.

Because Bast was pissed. "You didn't choose me," Bast said.

"I—" John sputtered, exasperated. "I'm still *here*. We got it all. I let it roll and my number came up."

"Yeah," Bast said, not happy.

"What's wrong with you?"

"You let it roll. You let me roll. You let *us* roll. You scared the piss out of me. It was a huge fucking gamble, and it wasn't just about you."

"You. You're thinking about you."

"I'm thinking I can't live without you. You have become the center of my existence. You're everything I want to live for. I can't go on sucking down evil, not without something wonderful to make it worth it. You can't show me the sun and then tell me I have to live forever underground."

"Read my mind."

"Why?"

"I want you to know what I was thinking last night."

"Tell me. Talk to me."

"Okay. Here it is. I don't want to be a loup-garou."

Bast crushed his eyes shut, his lips tight. John saw a tremor in his chin.

John went on. "I don't want to be a loup-garou with organ damage. I want to live as a man. I wanted to give the miracle a shot." Bast's eyes were still shut. John said, "And I decided if I made it to morning and no miracle showed up, I would go with you. I'd be the wolf."

Bast's eyes opened.

"I like to be needed," John said.

"That does seem to be your MO," Bast said shakily. "But you do realize you waited too long."

"I didn't," John said. Then, "Did I?"

"Those piles of ash you see in the rearview mirror are your bridges as of five o'clock this morning. The moon is waning."

"Well, hell. I'm glad I didn't know that."

John woke up. He didn't know why. He wasn't in that much pain.

His door was open a sliver. Light spilling in from the hospital corridor gave the room a look of dark twilight. Bast was sleeping, his head resting beside John's pillow on the bed.

Bast looked so young with his beautiful face relaxed, his full lips slightly parted. The beginning of a downy beard shadow darkened his jaw.

A motion drew John's eyes toward the wall, to the mirror there. The sliver of light, reflecting from the hall, blinked as if someone had walked past his room.

No one had.

John held his breath to listen for someone moving about. He heard only the steady beep of a machine somewhere, and the hiss of his own oxygen pump.

The sliver of light in the mirror blinked again. John stared as the roiling black shape moved in the glass—a reflection of nothing. John knew there was something in the room, something he couldn't see. Only the mirror showed it to him.

The mirror went black.

John's pulse leapt. He reached for the nightstand, fumbling at the drawers, scrambling for the lighter Bast had given him to protect against shadows. He pushed his tubes out of his way.

The tubes.

John had oxygen tubes in his nose. Fire would burn his face off. He couldn't see the shadow anymore. It was still in here. He knew it. He rasped, "*René!*"

Bast was awake and upright in an instant. He didn't ask anything. He commanded John in a harsh whisper, "Close your mouth and nose. And close your eyes!"

John immediately shut his mouth and pinched his nose between his forefinger and thumb. The oxygen softly buffeted at his closed nostrils.

The wolf leapt. John closed his eyes tight. Air rushed past his face. He heard the scritch of claws on the floor.

He'd been afraid to inhale before he closed his mouth. He didn't know where the shadow was. Now he needed to breathe. Right now. He kept holding his breath. It grew heavy in his lungs, and started to burn.

A dry, prickling sensation gripped his tightly clamped lips and nostrils. A grunt sounded, trapped in his throat. His head buzzed. Red shapes swarmed before his tight-shut eyes.

Then a feeling of moist heat, like the breath of a large animal, swept across his face.

His lungs ached. He really had to breathe. His heart raced, his pulse thundering in his ears. Even if he could hold on, one of those alarms on that monitor machine was going to start shrieking any second.

A warm hand pulled his hand away from his nose. Bast whispered, "It's gone."

John inhaled huge. His chest heaved. He exhaled long, then took a couple normal breaths, as he listened to his heartbeat slow down. The ringing in his ears subsided. "You got it."

"Yeah," Bast said. His breath smelled exceptionally bad.

John blinked against the smell. "Holy crap."

Bast went to the bathroom. John heard him in there, using some of the hospital mouthwash. Bast came back to the bedside and drank some of John's water. He exhaled into his cupped hand to check his breath.

"Why was it here?" John whispered.

"That was the shadow that shot you. The one that was in the majordomo. The shadows are after me. They know how to get to me now. I'm sorry I got you into this. I should go." He crouched to retrieve his trousers from the floor.

"Now who's talking like a March hare?" John said.

Bast pulled on his trousers and zipped up. "I can't let them get you." He picked up his long-sleeved polo shirt.

John watched him dressing. "You said you can't live without me."

Bast stopped what he was doing and held his shirt in his fists as if wringing it, his face directed toward the floor. He mumbled, "I can't."

"So what? You're going to go away and die?"

Silence answered.

John opened his arms. "Come here, you absolute idiot."

Bast let his shirt drop and he made his way through all the tubing to take John's embrace.

***

John looked at his abdomen as the dressing was changed. It didn't look near as bad as he'd expected. The surgeon had done his artistic best on a police officer wounded in the line of duty.

Bast visited every evening.

John was up and walking around sooner than he ever expected, pushing his metal tree hung with bags of fluids up and down the hall.

The surgeon, very pleased with his work, stopped in to see John. John asked, "So when can I get out of here?"

"Three more weeks."

"No."

"We need to watch for rejection."

"I'm not going to reject these organs. I like these organs and they like me. We're very happy together. Let us out of here."

The surgeon smiled at him and nodded agreeably. "In three weeks."

"Then I can go back to work," John said.

"In five more months, yes, probably."

"No," John said. That couldn't be right. "*Months?*"

"That part *may* go slightly faster for you. You were in perfect health before you landed in my operating room. Not the usual kind of patient I see."

"Oh, for God's—Doc, you gotta let me out of here."

The surgeon shook an immaculately manicured finger at him. "I did superb work on you. Don't screw it up."

In the middle of the third week of John's hospital stay, John's in-room phone rang. John reached for it. "Hamdon."

A cheery voice on the other end asked, "You still collecting bullets, Hammer?"

"Rossi! How the hell are you?"

Rossi was John's former partner and Daniel's godfather.

"I call with tidings of comfort and joy."

"Yeah?"

"The Feds got your buddy, Lloyd Crofton."

John tried to sit up. Mistake. He relaxed his abdomen. "What charge?"

"Attempted banking fraud. He got caught with his fingers in the wrong cookie jar. There's going to be paperwork coming your way."

"*My* way? Why?"

"It was Danny's bank account he tried to cash out."

The 35K life insurance payout. John never thought about it. The account was in John's name but Rossi knew where that money came from.

Rossi said, "Crofton had all your statistics, SSN, birth date, mother's maiden name."

"Now, where on earth would my ex-wife's husband get that kind of information?" John said acidly.

"Yeah. He had a photo ID. His photo, your stats. He's been practicing your signature because it was a nice forgery he signed."

"Then what was the giveaway?"

"An older gal at the bank knew you. She set up the account for you."

"Ma Sikorski."

"Her."

Against Ma's protests John had made the deposit into a non-interest-bearing checking account so he wouldn't receive interest statements on it. Seeing those would reopen the wound. He wanted to forget the damned thing's existence.

The life insurance policy had a purpose after all. It took Lloyd Crofton down. John had wanted him dead. It had taken everything John had not to murder Lloyd for letting his little boy die. And John would have done it too, if it would bring Daniel back. This was better.

He laughed. It hurt, but he couldn't stop.

And he fit that jagged piece of his life into a place in his heart where it didn't cut so deeply. Nothing horrendous could ever happen to his boy again. Everything had happened. It was all fixed in time now. And most of it was good. Daniel was safe now, forever young. John hoped there were puppies in heaven. Daniel always wanted a puppy. *I miss you, son. Love you. I'll see you later.*

Leaves on the trees were changing color. Regular season football games were on the TV.

The discharge nurse warned John against overdoing it. "Consider yourself on parole, Detective." She gave him the written instructions for taking care of himself. "And everyone asks, so I'll give you the answer right now, yes, you can have sex."

"I wasn't going to ask permission," John said.

John went home with Bast. Bast had moved most of John's stuff over from John's apartment into his Cajun red house.

Madonna, the white wolf, had done some redecorating. Screens were torn, and carpets had fringed edges they never had before. But as soon as John moved in, she turned into the sweetest, most respectful animal John had ever met.

She'd finished eating her hoard of bones, and though she didn't show it in her sides yet, she looked contentedly pregnant.

"How long is she going to carry her man-puppy?" John asked.

"Francois says nine months. Then we'll have a wolf pup for two or three years. Then." Bast stopped significantly.

John picked up that line. "Then we'll have a full-grown wolf man on our hands who thinks Dolly Madison is the first lady of the United States and not a snack cake. What is he going to *do*? He won't have Katrina to blame for his missing birth certificate."

"Francois knows an outfit in Wyoming that builds pasts for our kind. It's run by werewolves, but they'll take loup-garou too."

"You have got to be shittin' me," John said.

"*I* was surprised," Bast said.

John walked into the bedroom, took off his tee-shirt, and lay across the bed. He patted the mattress in front of him, inviting Bast to join him.

Bast stood in the bedroom door. "Are you sure it's not too soon?"

"It's way past due," John said.

Bast climbed onto the bed and approached him at a prowl on hands and knees. "You're not supposed to push it."

"Who you talkin' to? You know I'm gonna push it." He welcomed Bast under his arm. They lay face to face. They breathed each other's breaths. Their lips met. Bast traced John's mouth with the tip of his tongue.

John unfastened the buttons of Bast's shirt. "Bast?"

"John?"

"Stop looking at my scars," John said.

Bast's eyes kept straying downward.

"Kiss my ass," Bast said. He got up and stripped down to nothing but skin.

John watched him, captivated. Bast's beautiful body with his long limbs moved like a waking dream. Bast climbed back onto the bed, kneeling at the edge of it, his bare ass waiting at cock height.

John rolled off the mattress, grabbed the lube out of the nightstand, got rid of his jeans, and he circled the bed to stand behind Bast. He moved his hands adoringly over Bast's hard buttocks and the backs of his firm thighs. He crouched down and pressed his lips to either cheek, then stood back up and smoothed scented oil into Bast's ass cleavage. John slid his cock in the channel, back and forth. He breathed in cinnamon.

Bast reached back between his thighs to fondle John's balls. His touch sent John flying. Bast took John's cock in his hand and guided it to his anus. John pushed. Bast's body yielded to him, and surrounded him with heat. John moved back and forth, slowly at first, then faster in growing urgency. He felt the strain in Bast's long body between his hands. Bast's sides shone with sweat. His head tossed in rising passion. He was unbearably beautiful. His motions excited John, the pleasure between them mounting, thrust by needful thrust. John felt himself searing, soaring higher and higher to ignite into an all-consuming climax.

John rested on his back. Bast gazed down at John's face. He never wanted to be without that face. "Don't leave me, John."

"I don't intend to," John murmured.

"No. I mean it. Not ever."

"I mean it too," John said.

Bast's throat felt tight. He didn't want to push John away, but Bast would rather die than condemn his beloved to this kind of life unless John knew exactly what he was choosing. "You know how I live," he reminded John solemnly.

"Yeah. I do. It sucks. I still don't want to be a loup-garou. Your breath smells like asphalt after you inhale one of those shadows."

"Brimstone," Bast said, feeling faint. He was losing this man, this dear man.

John went on. "But as soon as I'm back to strength, you're gonna bite me under a full moon and I'm gonna chase shadows with you 'til the very last inning."

Bast gave a small gasp of incredible wonder. Baseball games had no limit on the number of innings and no time limit. They went on and on and on until someone won. Bast scarcely dared say, "You said you didn't want to be loup-garou."

"It's an ugly job, but you're right, I'm a rescuer. I'm not doing anything in this world if I'm not defending someone. I don't want anyone else to go through what Lori did. I want to kill Hitler. Shadows destroyed my best friend," John said. "They tried to kill my lover, they tried to get me. René, you're doing something important here and someone's gotta keep you out of trouble, 'cause you're not getting that part done yourself. And here's the thing—the bottom line—I love you. That's everything."

Bast kept from saying something idiotic like *Really?* John was right. Love was everything.

"It's you and me, René, for better and worse."

Bast was struck speechless. He put his arms around John, and pressed his face to the side of John's head and held him close. John's arms slid warmly around him. "Are you crying, René?"

"No." Bast licked his own tears off John's ear. He hadn't cried for happiness in a lifetime. He felt a sense of arrival, of being home at last—not home as a place—home at this man's side, wherever that should be, whenever. He was not alone anymore. He had his tough, steady lover to make this strange life of chasing shadows worth living.

And for the first time in an eternally long time, life wasn't just worth living. It was beautiful again.

The End

Chasing Shadows